'We'll see.' Zarios smiled. 'Till I do, you will be my fiancée. You will move in to my home so that I can take care of you— or rather deal with the press and the questions…'

'We won't…' Emma flushed. 'I mean, there'll be no…'

'I don't understand what you are saying…' He flashed her an innocent smile.

'Oh, I think you do. I want to make it clear, *very* clear, that we won't be sharing a bed.'

His mouth was mere inches from hers. Her mind was quailing, but her treacherous body flared in instant recall of their one dizzy time together.

'Do you want me to kiss you?'

Yes.

She didn't say it, but the word snapped like a twig between them.

She wanted to forget, to escape…for just one moment. To forget this living hell and taste the heaven she had once witnessed, to accept the temporary relief his mouth would surely provide.

To be held instead of holding up.

He kissed her then, his mouth crushing hers. And she was kissing him back with all her might, pressing her body into his as if she wanted to climb inside him, to escape, revelling in the freedom that his touch, his kiss, his *being* somehow brought her. Oh, she was lost, lost, lost—and it was wonderful. She was back in oblivion and it tasted divine.

Carol Marinelli recently filled in a form where she was asked for her job title, and she was thrilled, after all these years, to be able to put down her answer as 'writer'. Then it asked what Carol did for relaxation, and after chewing her pen for a moment Carol put down the truth—'writing'. The third question asked—'What are your hobbies?' Well, not wanting to look obsessed or, worse still, boring, she crossed the fingers on her free hand and answered 'swimming and tennis'. But—given that the chlorine in the pool does terrible things to her highlights, and the closest she's got to a tennis racket in the last couple of years is watching the Australian Open—I'm sure you can guess the real answer!

Carol also writes for Medical™ Romance!

BEDDED FOR PLEASURE, PURCHASED FOR PREGNANCY

BY
CAROL MARINELLI

MILLS & BOON

Pure reading pleasure™

All the characters in this book have no existence outside the imagination
of the author, and have no relation whatsoever to anyone bearing the
same name or names. They are not even distantly inspired by any
individual known or unknown to the author, and all the incidents are
pure invention.

First published in Great Britain 2009
Harlequin Mills & Boon Limited,
Eton House, 18-24 Paradise Road, Richmond, Surrey TW9 1SR

© Carol Marinelli 2009

ISBN: 978 0 263 87214 9

Set in Times Roman 10½ on 12¾ pt
01-0609-45736

Printed and bound in Spain
by Litografia Rosés, S.A., Barcelona

BEDDED FOR PLEASURE, PURCHASED FOR PREGNANCY

CHAPTER ONE

'GUESS who's coming tonight!'

Emma smiled at the excitement in her mother's voice as Lydia Hayes replaced the phone receiver.

'Half of Melbourne are coming!'

The party was all her mother had spoken about for the past few weeks, Emma's father's sixtieth birthday, and the intimate dinner they had initially planned had swelled to marquee proportions! Every inch of their sweeping bay view home had been commandeered to maximum effect, with the marquee open to reveal Port Phillip Bay in all its glory, and even the weather had obliged, with a clear sky allowing for city views. The dance floor had been laid, the band was setting up, caterers were milling, and Lydia was rattling with nerves as the hour approached. But the telephone call had, momentarily at least, halted her nerves.

'We've got an unexpected guest!' Lydia clasped her hands in delight. 'Go on, Emma, guess who.'

'Mum…' Emma wailed, wrapped in a towel and painting her toenails. Having spent the day helping her mother prepare, she was already racing against the clock to be ready.

'Just tell me.'

'Zarios!'

A smudge of red nail varnish streaked across Lydia's little toe. Pulling out a cotton bud, she dabbed at the area, refusing to let on that it mattered a jot that Zarios was coming tonight.

Oh, but it did.

Zarios—the single word that sent a tingle up every woman's spine. A man who didn't need to use his high-profile surname to be instantly recognisable.

His scowling but effortlessly beautiful face often appeared in the gossip columns. His reputation with women was appalling—so much so that it was a wonder, after so many blistering articles written on the man, that any woman might even *consider* getting involved with him.

Oh, but they did—over and over they did. And without fail it always ended in tears—or, to be more exact, the woman's tears.

'Why?' Curiosity got the better of Emma, and, screwing back the top on her nail varnish, she just couldn't stop herself asking.

Their fathers might be best friends, but why would Zarios D'Amilo even entertain the thought of coming to her father's celebration? Shouldn't he be sleeping with some supermodel on a Saturday night? Or crossing the equator on the way to some exclusive star-studded function? Certainly not on his way to celebrate Eric Hayes's sixtieth birthday.

Rocco D'Amilo had arrived in Australia nearly half a century ago, at eleven years of age. The son of Italian immigrants, he had been teased and goaded in his first hellish days at school. Unable to speak English, his lunchbox full of smelly meat, he had been an easy target, until Eric Hayes, who had suffered his own share of teasing in his time, had blackened the eye of the ringleader. The unlikely pair had been firm friends ever since.

Rocco had started out his working life as a builder, Eric as a real estate agent, and they had remained in touch even when Rocco had taken his young bride and new baby son back to Italy. They had been best man at each other's weddings, godparents at christenings, and their friendship had been the support Rocco needed when his young wife had walked out on her husband and four-year-old child.

Eric had done well for himself over the years and a few wise property investments meant his family lived comfortably. He had followed the 'worst house, best street' rule, and had bought a rundown home on a rundown acre in an exclusive beachside suburb, refurbishing it slowly until it gleamed with the same majesty as its view. Rocco, too, had achieved success, both here and in Rome, yet it was his son Zarios who had turned the family business into the empire it was today. His father's strong work ethic, combined with a private school education and a brilliant brain, had proved a dizzying recipe for success.

Zarios had emerged from university with big plans, which he had rapidly implemented, turning the modest but successful building company into a global property and finance company. D'Amilo Financiers had multiple branches throughout Europe and Australia and was stretching its golden fingers ever further across the globe. Now, with Rocco's retirement imminent, Zarios was expected to officially take the helm.

If only he would behave!

'He's on a final warning!' Even though there were only the two of them in the room, Lydia spoke in a loud whisper. 'Your father was telling me that apparently the board are sick of Zarios's caddish ways. They're uncomfortable with the prospect of him being the majority shareholder...'

'That's up to Rocco, surely...?' Emma frowned.

'Rocco's fed up with him, too. He's given that boy everything, and look how Zarios repays him. If the rest of the directors band together...' Lydia's voice lowered another octave '...and it sounds as if they might now. If the rumours that Zarios has split up with Miranda are true—she was his one saving grace.'

'They were only going out four months!' Emma pointed out.

'Which is a long time in dog years!'

Oh, how they laughed at that.

Emma's parents infuriated her at times—most of the time, in fact. The blatant preference they had for Emma's brother Jake, the way they repeatedly dismissed her career choice, as if by being an artist she didn't have a real job, and yet she adored them. Her mother was, and always had been to Emma, the funniest woman she knew.

And wrapped in a towel, doubled over in laughter as her mother hooted with mirth and the early evening sun dipped lower over the bay, drenching the living room in gold, somehow, on some level, Emma knew that this moment was precious.

She could have had no idea how precious, rich and good life was that gorgeous summer evening. No idea how many times she'd find herself playing it over and over again.

'Come on!' Dabbing her eyes, Lydia hurried her daughter up. 'Where on earth can I put him?'

'He's staying the night?' Emma's eyes widened at the very thought of Zarios D'Amilo sleeping here in this house.

'Yessss!' Lydia hissed, the joking well and truly put aside now, as her already high stress levels rocketed. 'I knew Rocco was—but Zarios! He'll have to have your room!'

'He jolly well won't.'

'We can hardly give him the trundle bed in the study—Jake's squeezed into his old room, Rocco's in the guestroom…Zarios will *have* to have yours. Come on, it's time to get dressed,' Lydia said, refusing to debate the point, buoyed at the prospect of having such a high-profile guest. 'My friends are going to simply *die* with jealousy—can you imagine Cindy's face when she finds out? You did buy something nice for tonight, I hope?'

'Like a bridal gown?' Emma said, firmly tongue in cheek.

'Well, he *has* broken up with Miranda!'

Emma's sarcasm was entirely wasted on her mother. Lydia Hayes had spent her married life clinging on to the middle rung of the social ladder, and was determined that her children would rise to the heights she had never achieved.

'Australia's most eligible bachelor is joining us to celebrate your father's sixtieth birthday, Emma. Surely you're just a little bit excited?'

'Of course I'm excited.' Emma smiled. 'About Dad's birthday…'

'Get ready, then,' Lydia chided, and then, wincing

slightly, massaged her temples. 'They'll be arriving soon…'

'Mum, calm down.'

'What if they're expecting something spectacular?'

'Then we'll wheel out Zarios!' Emma smiled again, but her mother was past jokes. 'They're expecting a birthday celebration, which this *is*,' Emma said, walking across the lounge and taking her mother's hands from her temples and holding them. 'They're coming to see you and Dad. That's all that matters.'

'Jake's not even here yet!' Lydia trilled. 'My own son can't make it on time. Do you think he'll have remembered to order the pastries for breakfast?' Emma could hear panic once again creeping into her mother's voice and moved quickly to avert it.

'Of course he'll have remembered. You go and sort out fresh sheets for my bed, and I'll go and get ready. *And*,' she added with a wry smile, 'I'll give my room a quick tidy!'

Her bedroom was exactly the same as it had been seven years ago, when she'd left home to go to university to study art. Emma loved coming back and staying in her old room, amongst her old familiar things, but this evening she eyed it somewhat critically, wondering what Zarios would make of the paintings that adorned the walls, the curtains she had tye-died herself when she was twelve, the tatty overfilled bookshelves and the dressing table laden with childhood photos.

Emma had always intended to wear *something nice* for her father's special night. Her tiny broom cupboard of an art gallery was in Chapel Street in Melbourne, and as well as her gallery the street boasted an array of designer boutiques. Slipping on the cerulean blue dress, Emma wondered what on earth had possessed her. It had caught her eye in the window—the shade of blue almost a replica of the view of the bay from her parents' balcony. The price had been an instant dissuader, yet the assistant had suggested Emma at least try it on. Staring at her reflection, Emma let her teeth worry away at her bottom lip as she wondered if it wasn't just a bit too much.

Or too little!

An inch shorter than she would have preferred, it clung provocatively in all the wrong places. Her bottom surely appeared massive, and her breasts as if they had instantly gone up a size, where the feather-light wool caressed her figure, only loosening its grip at mid-thigh, then hanging innocently, yet flaring as smoothly as a trumpet bell as she walked.

It was, quite simply, divine.

Worthy, Emma told herself as she pulled a shoebox from her case, of the horribly expensive strappy sandals she'd bought to go with it. Worthy of the hours of buffing and polishing her body had endured—and her first visit to a tanning parlour.

Running her ceramic straighteners for the final time over her long blonde hair, she stopped worrying her bottom lip and applied a final layer of lipgloss instead, thanking the gods who had looked after her these past days, who must have known that Zarios D'Amilo would be coming tonight, and had, unbeknown to Emma, insisted that she look her best for the embarrassing task of facing him again after all these years.

Emma picked up one of the photos on her dressing

table and stared at the wedding group. Even though it
was ridiculous, even though it was only a photo, still she
blushed as she looked into Zarios's serious dark eyes.

She'd been nineteen…

A young and extremely naive nineteen-year-old, she
had been dressed up like a vast pink blancmange, as
bridesmaid at Jake's wedding.

Zarios had been invited. He'd only been in Australia
a few weeks back then, and his accent had been so
heavy and rich Emma had struggled to understand his
words—except she could have listened to him talk for
ever. Put simply, he had been the most stunning man she
had ever seen. The whole wedding had passed in a dizzy
blur until finally, dutifully, he had danced with her. And
because it had been Zarios D'Amilo holding her, and
she'd had rather too much champagne, Emma had
promptly fallen in lust.

Shoving the photo in a drawer, she turned it face-down
and covered it with the drawer's contents, then slammed
it closed. The last thing she wanted was for Zarios to see
it—for Zarios to recall her exquisitely embarrassing mistake. But even with the photo safely tucked away Emma
was struggling to beat her blush, struggling to banish the
image of the two of them dancing that night. Zarios had
lowered his head to say something and stupidly, blindly,
she'd misinterpreted the action, closed her eyes and, lips
poised, waited expectantly for him to kiss her.

Even six years on she burnt with the shame of the
memory.

Could still hear his deep, throaty laugh as he'd realised
what she thought he had intended.

'Come back when you're all grown up…' He'd smiled

at her and patted her bottom as the music had ended, merrily sending her on her childish way. 'Anyway, my father would never forgive me.'

He'd probably forgotten, Emma consoled herself.

With all the women he'd dated, as if he'd remember a teenager's clumsy attempt at extracting a kiss. Anyway, she was six years older now and light years wiser—she could see a man like Zarios exactly for what he was: a player.

She certainly wouldn't make the same mistake again; she'd be aloof and distant, Emma decided, practising an aloof and distant look in the mirror. Maybe she should wear her hair up? Emma thought, piling her long blonde hair on her head and seeing if it made a difference, then deciding against. Maybe she should just make a joke about it, laugh the whole thing off...

Maybe she should tidy her room!

Her mother joined her, and the embroidered quilt was hastily replaced with crisp white linen as Lydia ran around the room removing stray bras, mascara wands and tampon boxes. Folded towels and washcloths were placed at the end of the bed, along with a little bar of Lydia's expensive soap, and a jug of water and a glass was put beside the bed, covered with a little linen cloth.

'It's mineral water,' Lydia assured a bemused Emma as she arranged the jug with precision. 'Should I put out a little snack for him?' she worried. 'Is there anything else you can think of?'

'A box of tissues?' Emma nudged her mother, making Lydia giggle again. 'Legend has it he can't go twelve hours!'

But even if she could make her mother laugh and

relax just a touch, as she stared out at the bay Emma felt her throat tighten when she heard a helicopter approach and knew it was him. As comfortably off as her parents and their friends might be, only the D'Amilos would arrive for a party in a helicopter. She watched it hover for a moment, could see the marquee flapping, the grass flattened by the whirring blades, and then...

She knew she was holding her breath, because the window had stopped misting over, and she knew as one well-shod foot appeared, followed by an impossibly long leg, that it was *him*.

The view only improved from that point.

Zarios helped his father down, then, having ducked under the blades, they strolled across the lawn, too used to their mode of travel to give the helicopter even a backward glance as it lifted off into the sunset.

He was wearing black dress pants and a fitted white shirt, and like a prize thoroughbred being paraded before the race he had a restless energy, a glossy, groomed appearance, that had Emma's stomach fold in on itself as he tossed his head back and laughed at something his father said. For just a moment, an embarrassing twinge, Emma was sure he saw her. Those black eyes had glanced up as if he knew he was being watched, and Emma stepped quickly back, as if burnt.

'Emma!' She could hear her mother's shrill summons and, taking a deep breath, she steadied herself. 'They're here! An hour early and they're *here*!'

'Questi sono i miei buoni amici.' As they walked across the lawn, again his father reminded him how important these people were to him.

'You believe too much of what you read!' Zarios laughed. 'I *am* capable of behaving occasionally. Anyway, I fear it will be slim pickings at a sixtieth birthday bash, Pa!'

'Zarios…' Rocco was serious. It had seemed like a good idea for him to bring Zarios. Fresh out of a relationship, Zarios had that gleam in his roving eye that spelt danger—and if Rocco could avert scandal at this precarious time, then he would. Ah, but had it been wise to bring him here? On the short flight over Rocco had remembered the wedding, the instant attraction that had flared between his son and Emma Hayes. He had warned Zarios off that night—and thankfully the warning had been heeded. But Zarios was six years older now, and way past taking his father's advice. 'You remember their daughter, Emma?'

'The good-looking blonde?' A smile flickered across his face in instant recall. Things were maybe looking up for tonight after all. 'Actually, I do.'

'She's grown into a very attractive woman…'

'Splendid!'

'*Attesa!*' Rocco called for his son to slow down, pulling out his handkerchief and mopping his brow.

'Are you okay, Pa?'

'A little chest pain…' Rocco took a pill from a little silver box and placed it under his tongue. 'Nothing I am not used to.' He *did* have chest pain—perhaps not enough to merit taking a pill, but if the sympathy card would help Rocco was only too willing to play it. 'You know I think the world of Lydia, but you know how she loves to spend—and, well, it would seem that Emma has the same tendency…'

'It is fortunate I am rich then, no?' Zarios joked, but his father wasn't smiling.

'Eric is worried…' It was only a small lie, Rocco consoled himself. In fact he hadn't lied, he told himself, just implied… Surely it was better to put Zarios off now, than face Eric after his son had broken his daughter's heart?

And he would, Rocco thought wearily, mopping his forehead again before folding his handkerchief and putting it back in his pocket. Zarios *would* break her heart.

'Don't get involved with her, Zarios.' Rocco resumed his walking. 'It would be far too messy.'

'You're early!' Eric, as laid-back as his wife was neurotic, didn't worry about things like guestrooms and final layers of lipgloss, instead he was simply delighted as Rocco came through the door, and hugged and embraced his lifelong friend in the effusive Italian way. Zarios stood slightly back.

'We wanted some time with you before the other guests arrived.' Rocco beamed, offering Eric a lavishly wrapped gift. 'Hide that and open it tomorrow.'

'The invitation said no gifts!' Lydia scolded, but she was clearly delighted that he had. 'Zarios—we're *thrilled* that you came.'

'It is good to be here.'

His accent was still rich, his voice low and deep, and Emma could feel the tiny hairs at the back of her neck stand on end as she came down the stairs, attempting to maintain her distant and aloof look, watching as he kissed her mother on both cheeks and then did the same with her father. His black eyes met hers.

'Emma. It's been a long time.' His smile was guarded, and in a split second his eyes took in the changes. The short cut she had once worn had long since grown out, and her hair now hung in a heavy blonde curtain over her shoulders. Her once skinny, overactive body had softened and filled out since then, too, and her feminine curves were enhanced by the soft drape of her dress— a dress that swished around her slender legs as she moved. Zarios was surprisingly grateful for his father's warning, because without it the night might have taken a rather different direction.

She had always been pretty, but she was stunning now!

'It *has* been a long time.' She walked down the last two steps and hovered on the bottom one, but still he had to bend his head to kiss her on the cheeks. As he did so, he smelt her—*again*. His body flared in surprised recognition as his lips dusted her cheeks. How nice it would be, Zarios thought wildly, to give her the kiss he had denied her so many years ago.

Had denied *himself*.

The others moved forward, leaving them alone for just a moment, each lost in their own thoughts.

'You are looking well.' He frowned slightly. 'How long has it been since we've seen each other?'

'A few years?' Emma shrugged, refusing to acknowledge she knew the exact length of time, down to the month! 'Four—maybe five?'

'It's not that long...' Zarios shook his head as they headed through to the lounge. 'It was at your brother's wedding.'

'That was five years ago...' Emma smiled. 'Actually, it was six!'

'Come through,' Lydia scolded. 'Emma, get our guests a drink.'

At that moment one of the hired help arrived with a hastily filled tray of champagne. Emma grabbed one for herself before Lydia shooed her away.

'A real drink!' Lydia hissed to Emma out of the side of her mouth.

'Whisky?' Emma checked. That was what Rocco always had when he came over. 'And a small dash of water?'

'She has a good memory.' Rocco beamed.

'Zarios?' Emma deliberately forced herself to look him in the eye. 'What would you like?' Black eyes held hers, and she could have sworn there was just a fraction of innuendo in the pause that went on for just a beat too long. The torch she had carried for him over the years flared brightly as his eyes held hers, no matter how she tried to douse it.

'Whisky.' He added no please or thank you to his order. 'No water.'

And as easily as if he'd flicked a switch she was lost.

Pouring the golden liquid, she could see her hand was shaking. She hadn't exaggerated the memory of him. He *was* as lethal and as potently sexy as he had been all those years ago—and as arrogant and rude, Emma reminded herself. Handing him his glass, trying and failing not to notice the brush of his fingers against hers, she crossed the room and sat on the sofa, as far away from him as possible.

The cat soon found the mouse.

He sat beside her, just a tiny bit too close for her liking. There was no contact, none at all, but she could feel the heat from his body, feel the weight of him, the ancient springs in the leather couch tilting her just a fraction towards him.

He invaded her space—but perhaps that was his trick. No one watching could testify to intrusion; you had to be beside him, or looking at him, to feel it. Taking a sip of her champagne, she wished she had chosen whisky, too—wished for something, anything, strong enough to douse the nerves that were leaping like salmon in her chest.

'I take it Jake and his wife will be coming tonight?'

'Just Jake.' Emma gave a tight smile.

'They have twins now, don't they?' Zarios checked, watching her closely, seeing the brittle smile on her face slip into a more relaxed one as she described her niece and nephew.

'Harriet and Connor—they'll be three in a few weeks' time.' On cue her brother arrived, bustling into the room.

'Darling!' Lydia practically fell on to her son's neck, the lateness of his arrival immediately forgiven. 'It's *so* good to see you.'

'Sorry, sorry…' Jake beamed. 'The traffic was an absolute nightmare.'

'On a Saturday?' Emma couldn't help herself.

'The football's on!' Lydia beamed. 'The city's hell around this time—it's just wonderful you made it, darling. You did remember the pastries for tomorrow…?'

There was a tiny, appalling pause as Jake's fixed smile slipped just a fraction, his frantic eyes darting to his sister. Lydia's mouth opened in horror mid-sentence. Emma was almost tempted not to intervene, to refuse to save the day yet again for her brother and let them see that the *one* thing, the one thing he had been asked to contribute, had proved too much for him. But, as Jake well knew, she couldn't do that to her parents.

'Oh, I forgot to tell you, Mum—the bakers rang to confirm Jake's order. They'll be here first thing.'

'Oh, Emma!' her mother snapped. 'You could have let me know!'

'Where is Beth?' Rocco frowned, voicing the question Lydia had clearly hoped he wouldn't. 'And where are the twins? I was looking forward to seeing them again.'

'Tonight's for adults only.' Lydia beamed again, but there was a rigid set to her lips.

'Why?' Rocco had been single too long, and missed the warning signs flashing from Lydia's eyes to simply drop it. 'Children are part of the family…they should be here…'

Surprisingly, it was Zarios who saved the day.

'Oh, come on, Pa…' Zarios gave a thin smile, and Emma was sure there was just a flash of contempt as he halted his father—could hear the slight drip of sarcasm in his expansive deep voice. 'Surely you remember how hard it is settling little ones to bed at a family function—and all those things you have to remember to bring?'

'Absolutely!' Lydia nodded furiously. 'We'll see the twins next weekend—oh, and Beth, of course…'

'Don't worry.' Zarios gave Emma a tight smile as the conversation drifted on. 'My father is a master of the "don't do as I do, do as I say" school of thought.'

'Meaning?'

'Nothing.' He took a slug of his whisky before concluding, 'It does not matter.'

Oh, but clearly it did!

He dismissed her frown with a shrug. 'It is strange

seeing my father in this setting—looking forward to seeing little children and catching up with friends. Usually the only time I socialise with my father is at work events…'

'And family—'

'No.' He cut her off, and she winced at her own insensitivity—her parents *were* Rocco's family. 'It is strange to see him amongst a family.'

She had always known that once his mother had left Zarios had been raised at a boarding school; her mother had told her how hard poor Rocco had had to work, jetting between the two countries to keep up with the fees, and how devastated poor Rocco had been when sometimes he couldn't get back to see Zarios.

Only then did it dawn on Emma—really dawn on her—that, as difficult as it might have been for *poor* Rocco, how much harder it must have been on his son.

CHAPTER TWO

STILL, Zarios didn't appear to be dwelling on it.

If he was here under sufferance he didn't show it—laughing at Eric's jokes, and making Lydia blush at every turn with his smouldering smile.

Suddenly the hour had arrived, and the small party moved into the marquee as the band started playing and the guest numbers began rapidly multiplying. Zarios was quickly cornered by Cindy, a good-looking blonde who was a good friend of her mother's. Emma knew she had to be nudging fifty, but years of botox and bulimia were serving her well tonight. Well, good luck, Emma thought, actually glad of the reprieve.

Zarios unsettled her.

Unsettled each fibre of her being.

Every flicker of his five-star reputation was merited. The question as to how any woman could dismiss such a heartbreak reputation had, for Emma, been well and truly answered—up close he was intoxicating.

Emma suppressed a smile as Cindy laughed a little too loudly at something he said, her hand resting on his arm as she spoke intently—she was welcome to him.

'Can I talk to you later, Emma?' Jake came over,

waving to a couple of geriatric aunts and smiling as if for cameras—just as he always did.

'Sure!'

'Away from everyone...' he added, and Emma's heart sank.

'Why?'

'Don't be like that.' Jake sighed.

'Are you going to pay me for the pastries?' If she sounded petty, it was with good reason. *If* Jake paid her maybe there would be nothing to worry about—maybe she *was* being surly for no reason.

She truly hoped that was the case.

'Look, I'm sorry about that.'

'Jake, it was the one thing Mum asked *you* to organise. What if I hadn't ordered them?'

'But you did!' Emma could have sworn there was a belligerent tone to his voice, but he quickly checked it. 'Here...' He pulled out his wallet and thrust her some notes. 'Thanks for organising them. I'll catch up with you later.'

'Can I ask what it's about?'

'Not here, okay?'

Not here, where everyone might find out that you're less than perfect, Emma thought savagely. But of course she didn't say it, just gave him a nod and bit hard on her lip, close to tears all of a sudden as Jake walked off.

'Jake.' Zarios raised his eyebrows in greeting as Jake brushed past, he'd seen the exchange and Jake must know it. The polite thing to do would be to ignore it, but Zarios couldn't be bothered with being polite. Shrugging off Cindy, he offered a friendly enquiry as Jake approached. 'Is everything okay?'

'All good!' Jake grinned, but his cheeks were red, his eyes following Zarios's gaze to his sister. 'Just family stuff. You know…'

'Not really,' Zarios answered.

'Just…' Both men stood watching as Emma slipped the money into her purse. 'Well, it's difficult for Emma. You help out when you can, you know?'

Yes, Zarios knew—and he knew now he should leave well alone. But his curiosity was well and truly piqued, and when a coo of delighted glee swept around the party as waiters and waitresses walked through with silver trays laden with finger food Zarios found himself making his way back to Emma.

'You're looking worried.'

Emma forced a rapid smile. 'I've no idea what my mother's cooked up for tonight.'

'Well, she's surpassed herself.'

Knowing how important keeping up appearances was for her mother, Emma was relieved to hear it. Glancing at the tray a waitress offered, she expected the usual variation on a theme. But a *real* smile formed on her full lips as she realised that for the first time, where the politics of entertaining were concerned, had listened to her own heart.

'Oh!' Emma blinked at the tray laden with tiny little sandwiches. The bread as thin and as light as butterfly wings, yet it was crammed with the strangest of filling choices for such an important function.

Jam.

Vegemite.

Salami.

Prosciutto.

All beautifully presented, of course, but as she bit into them the familiar flavours brought a gurgle of laughter to Emma's lips. She got the joke.

'Your father and mine used to swap their school lunches.' Zarios grinned, too. 'I can remember my father telling me the first time he tasted your father's sandwiches. He thought they were the most disgusting thing he had ever tasted—and your father thought the same of his. Within two weeks they were trading lunches.'

'My dad insists he was the first Australian to really appreciate a sundried tomato—he was eating them daily long before they were popular.'

'He was,' Zarios agreed. 'He was also a friend to my father when no one else was. He's a good man.'

'He is.' Emma smiled. 'Which is why you'll have to excuse me. I ought to socialise…'

'You are.'

'I mean…' Emma was flustered '…with aunts and things…'

'I'm sure your father would rather you looked after a guest who doesn't know anyone…'

How dangerous was that smile, just curving on the edge of his full mouth?

'It's not fair to leave me on my own.'

'I'm sure Cindy would be delighted to keep you company!' *Ouch!* Emma could have kicked herself for letting him know that she'd noticed.

'Cindy only wants me for my body!' He leaned forward, his voice dropping an octave. Cool and confident Emma was not. Her face burned at the near contact, her toes curling in her sandals at the feel of his breath on her ear. 'And I will not let myself be used!'

'As if.' Emma laughed, jerking her head back, but the laugh came out too shrill. The effect of him so close was devastating.

'Anyway, I am under strict instructions to behave tonight…' Again he lowered his head—just as he had a moment ago, just as he had six years ago—and again her body demanded a kiss. 'I think Cindy has an issue with her age…' His Italian accent was thick, his words curious rather than mocking. 'Which puts me off.'

'Her age?' Emma checked, struggling to sound normal as he pulled her ever closer into his personal space.

'No, the fact that she has issues…' Zarios smiled. 'I am too much of a bastard to remember to be reassuring.'

God, he was gorgeous. Wicked and bad, but funny, too! Pulling her head back, holding out her glass for a waiter to top it up, Emma was sorely tempted to ask for the ice bucket to douse herself in.

He was thoroughly good company, and if his conversation was laced with innuendo, not once was he sleazy. And, Emma noticed with a shiver of nervous excitement, despite his arrogance it was with great skill and surprising kindness that he deflected the numerous attempts from women to garner his attention.

For tonight at least his sole focus was on her.

Her mother *had* excelled herself—and for Emma it really was a wonderful party. The mixture and the number of guests was perfect, the food delicious and the drinks plenty. Zarios continued to be good company, and had it not been for Jake, following her into the house and colliding with her as she came out of the toilet, it would have been perfect.

It wasn't good news—but then it never was with

Jake. As he led her to the study to *talk*, and as Emma listened to all he had to say, the sense of foreboding that had been her companion for a long time where Jake was concerned gave way to sheer incredulity at what he was asking of her. There was no way she could help him.

'Jake, I don't have that sort of money…'

'You could get it, though!'

'How?' Emma's eyes widened. 'You're talking about a six-figure sum.'

'Your flat's worth way more than you paid for it, Emma.'

'Why would I pay off your debts…again?' she couldn't help but add. She'd helped him out in the past and had never been paid back. She had chosen not to pursue it, but this was a ridiculous amount Jake was now asking for. 'Why would I take out yet another loan to help you?'

'Because if I don't get this sorted Beth will leave. Listen, Emma…' He dragged a hand through his hair. 'She hasn't worked in years, she moans about money all the time, and yet she does nothing to help out…'

'She's got two-year-old twins!' Emma pointed out angrily. 'Surely that's work enough?'

'Emma.' He dropped his voice so low she had to strain to catch it. 'Don't tell Mum and Dad—I don't want to worry them—but we're having problems with the twins…' As Emma bit on her lip, he continued. 'Behavioural problems. That's one of the reasons we didn't bring them tonight. Beth has no control—she can't even manage to get them dressed before lunch. You don't know what it's like, living with her. She doesn't lift a plate, she's at home all day and I'm still having to pay for a cleaner… Emma, if you don't help me and I lose the house, you can guarantee I'll lose the twins, too. Can you imagine Mum and Dad…?'

'You have to tell them, Jake,' Emma pleaded. 'You say it isn't gambling this time?'

'It isn't!' Jake promised. 'Just a lousy call on the stockmarket. Emma, it would kill Mum and Dad. They're so…'

'Proud?' Emma spat, because at this very moment she hated him—and hated, too, how easily her parents were fooled by him. Jake the golden boy. Jake the one with the *real* job. Jake who had given them the twins. Poor, responsible Jake, with his moody, depressed wife.

If only they knew.

'I'm due for a massive bonus at the end of June. If I don't tell Beth about it, I can pay you back then.'

'Lie to her again, you mean?'

'Help me, Emma.'

'I'll think about it.'

'Emma, please.'

'I'll think about it!' she said again, and it was the best she could offer.

Upset, worried, she marched out of the study, trying to get her head together before she faced the party that was still going on.

'Hey!' Zarios stepped back as she practically collided with him.

'Sorry…' Emma gave a quick shake of her head. 'I wasn't looking where I was going.'

'I'm trying to find where they put our cases. My father needs one of his tablets.'

'Of course.'

Flustered, Emma led him to the guestroom, her mind reeling too much from Jake's confession for her to be embarrassed at being alone upstairs with Zarios.

'They're not here.' She scanned the bedroom. 'They must be in my room...where you're sleeping,' Emma added as he followed behind.

'How very open-minded of your parents!'

'Daughter not included!' Emma gave a tight, distracted smile as she flung her bedroom door open. 'There they are. I'd better go down—the cake should be coming out soon.'

'Are you okay?'

No, she wanted to scream, but knew she couldn't. She just gave him a worried, confused nod.

'I'm fine.'

'If you want to talk...'

'Why would I talk to *you*?' Emma challenged. 'I hardly know you!'

'That can be sorted.' He gestured to the bedroom, but on turning back to her immediately Zarios shook his head at her stunned expression. 'I meant we could talk in private here...'

Only a fool would walk into a bedroom with Zarios and expect conversation! But for a second she was tempted.

Tempted to push his arrogant, testosterone-loaded body into the dark space. Tempted to be daring and wicked and reckless and...her rabid mind flailed as it tried to come up with the word—*bad*.

To for once be irresponsible—and, yes, very, *very* bad.

Only it wasn't Emma.

'As I said.' Ever the dutiful daughter, she gave him a brittle smile, then turned on her new and starting to rub high heels. 'They'll be bringing out the cake soon.'

* * *

She wished they *would* bring out the cake.

There was the most appalling lull—but only Emma seemed to notice.

The dance floor was still heaving with couples, the tables filled with chatting and laughing groups, but despite her best efforts to join in with a couple of conversations it was hard going.

Dutiful Jake was chatting up the old aunties and making them laugh, and Cindy's eyes had shot knives when Emma had attempted to join a group of women. All in all she'd left it too late to suddenly join in with the others. Everyone was settled in to their little cliques, making her feel like a wallflower. Then Zarios returned.

'Looks like you're stuck with me.'

He took her by the wrist, then led her to the dance floor without asking.

Which was a wise move on his part. Because had he asked, she would have declined—not because she didn't want to dance, but because of how much she did.

He held her loosely at first, swaying to the heavy beat as she willed her heart and breathing to slow down. The second they did, he pulled her closer.

Was it his looks or his status that made him so appealing? Emma begged to know as his arms snaked around her back. And was it just his reputation that held her back? All she knew was that it was a dizzying combination—want and trepidation, curiosity and nervousness, all there fizzing in each cell of the body he was holding.

'I don't like cake...' Zarios smiled down at her '...which gives us more time for dancing.'

'Oh, but my mother thinks of everything,' Emma quipped. 'I'm sure there'll be a fruit platter.'

'Forbidden fruit, perhaps?'

'I'm far from forbidden.' Emma gave a wry smile as her mother danced past them and practically fractured her father's rib as, none too subtly, she pointed out the lovely couple dancing, clearly delighted at to how well they were getting on. 'My mother lives for the day we might get together.'

'While my father shudders at the thought.'

All the ingrained insecurities of her childhood, all her mother's deepest fears seemed to seep into her pores. But as his hands spread around her waist and he pulled her just a fraction closer, Emma realised she'd misinterpreted him.

'He has told me many times that, though he would love nothing more than for us to be together... Well, he knows my reputation. He says he would not be able to look at your father if I were to hurt you.'

Her blue eyes jerked to his, her mind screaming for her to be quiet. But the words were out before she could stop them.

'Then don't.' It was the most blatant flirt—the most blatant acknowledgement of their attraction—but she recovered quickly. 'Anyway—given you're seeing Miranda...'

'We broke up.'

'I'm sorry.'

'I'm not.' He didn't miss a beat, either in dancing or flirting, his repertoire as sleek and practised as the body that moved with hers. 'Maybe we could have coffee or dinner when you are back in the city—somewhere away from our families' eyes...'

'Perhaps…' Emma nodded, trying to shrug, trying to pretend it didn't matter.

Oh, but it did.

'Is that a yes?'

'Yes…'

'I will ring.'

'Sure.' Somehow she managed a casual smile, but her heart was soaring as he pulled her in closer.

'I like your scent.'

'It's just…' She shrugged, tried to be casual, but for the life of her she couldn't remember the perfume's name. 'I got it for my birthday.'

'I meant *your* scent,' he corrected her, which made her cheeks burn.

She'd never been held like this. He was barely touching her, and they were barely moving, yet it was positively indecent the sensations he evoked. Her internal barometer had shattered, common sense scattering like tiny balls of mercury, irrecoverable as he pulled her right into the circle of his arms. His breath was hot on her ear and suddenly she wanted him to lick it—he didn't. Lowering his head just a bit further, till she could feel his mouth just inches from her neck, she fought the urge to repeat her mistake of yesteryear. She wanted to turn her face to his like a flower to the sun, to receive the sweet reward of his mouth on hers.

It was a relief when the music ended—a relief to stand apart from him in the darkness as the room broke into song.

Eric smiled broadly as a vast cake was wheeled in, blazing with sixty candles. Still Zarios held Emma's wrist, his hot fingers wrapped tightly around her flesh as she sang along. Then the candles were blown out and the tent was plunged into full darkness. Tonight she finally received what she'd longed for all those years ago and for way too many moments in between. Finally Emma was rewarded with the prize of his mouth on hers.

Even a vivid imagination couldn't adequately prepare her for the thoroughness of his kiss, the shocking feel of his tongue sliding into hers, the way his body enveloped hers. He tasted like manna, his scent potently male. It was a thrilling, decadent kiss that she *absorbed*—a kiss during which he pressed himself so hard into her she could feel the dangerous thick length of him. It was a kiss so consuming that it triggered a dangerous chain reaction—one that made her forget to breathe, forget to think, forget even herself.

If the entire embrace lasted only ten or maybe fifteen seconds it was just as well. Because any more and she'd have come there and then. His timing was impeccable, though, and by the time the last cheer had faded, before the cameras had stopped flashing, his mouth had released hers. She had to peel herself off him and stand in lights that were suddenly blazing. No one had seen them, all eyes were still on her father, yet she felt as if the spotlight was suddenly on *her*—that surely everyone knew what had just taken place. She felt as embarrassed, almost, as if they'd been caught making love—hell, she felt as if they *had* been making love. Her panties were damp with arousal, her nipples erect and throbbing beneath her soft dress; so exposed was her want, surely everyone could see it?

What did this man do to her?

She could see Rocco's eyes narrowing in disapproval, and her mother's questioning frown as she saw the glow in her daughter's cheeks.

Zarios *was* dangerous.

Bad and dangerous—yet irresistible.

It was nearly 2:00 a.m. by the time they all got to bed, and Emma was exhausted.

Peeling off her dress, only in reverence to its price tag did she bother to hang it over a chair in the study. And apart from a lethargic brush of her teeth, the rest of her nighttime routine went to pot. Climbing into the trundle bed in the study, Emma listened to the familiar sounds of the family home—her father coughing, the stairs creaking as her parents went to bed, the bark of a possum in a tree outside. It should have been soothing and familiar, and she was so tired she should have been asleep in a matter of seconds, but she was too aware that Zarios was *in situ*—that tonight he lay in her bed.

How she wished she were there!

Every creak of the floorboards, every turn of a tap, had her staring into the darkness at the door, terrified that he'd come in.

And she was shamefully, bitterly disappointed when he didn't.

CHAPTER THREE

EMMA didn't know what to do.

The sun wasn't up yet, and the silence of dawn was attempting to soothe her as Emma strode along the beach, her head racing at a thousand miles an hour after an angst-riddled sleepless night.

Damn Zarios for being so irresistible.

And damn her for being so willing.

Anyone might have seen him kissing her and pressing himself into her last night. If the lights had come on even a second earlier... Emma simultaneously cringed and soared at the memory, viewing it as if through parted fingers, wanting to see it, yet horribly embarrassed all the same.

He was a playboy, Emma told herself, walking quickly now. A bored playboy, stuck at a party he probably hadn't wanted to attend. A restless, oversexed male who'd been looking for diversion, for amusement—and she'd provided it.

Well, no more.

He'd be gone after breakfast and that would be the last she'd see of him.

Unless he called her!

Still, it wasn't just Zarios and his potent sex appeal that had her head spinning as she strode angrily through the still dawn. Damn Jake, too, for ruining her father's birthday for her.

If only her parents knew.

If only they knew the thin ice he perpetually skated on. Oh, their parents had helped Jake out a couple of times—when the stockmarket had supposedly taken a tumble, and when the twins were first born and Beth had been hospitalised with depression—but unbeknown to them she, too, had helped. Emma swallowed down the flutter of unease at the thought of the credit card account she had opened to bail him out, the personal loan she had taken… Each time Jake had promised he'd pay her back; each time he had sworn it would be the last…

…and each time he had lied.

Emma stared out at the grey morning, willing the sun to come up and shed some light on what she should do.

She didn't have the sort of money Jake needed.

Possibly she could get an extension on her mortgage. She'd always been so careful. She had lived frugally throughout her student years, even managing to set some money aside from casual jobs, and her father had found her a modest flat near where she rented the gallery—a flat that had increased in value. But her paintings weren't doing so well. She was still too new, too little known. Because of helping Jake she'd had to cut back on advertising, had had to forgo the promotional nights at her gallery that might draw in the customers.

Emma gulped. Why *should* she help him? If she gave him this money Emma knew that she'd never see it again—which should make saying no incredibly simple.

Only… She could almost feel the sting of her mother slapping her cheek all those years ago when, after another of Jake's so-called cries for help, Emma had voiced the same question. Why couldn't he *cope*?

'*He's ill, Emma!*'

Closing her eyes, she could see her mother's lips—pale, furious lips that had been spitting at the edges as she spoke. The slap had been less shocking than the fury that had accompanied it—her mother had been appalled at the question her seventeen-year-old daughter had raised.

'*You should try and be more understanding!*'

That had been their sole conversation regarding Jake's illness—no discussion, no acknowledgement. The memories of those black days had been filed and tucked away, by unspoken rule never to be opened.

But, try as her mother might, the lid was peeping open.

And, try as Emma might, this time she might not be able to stop it.

To swim alone on a deserted beach that was still draped in darkness broke every safety rule that had been ingrained into Emma from the moment she could walk and had toddled on little fat legs to the water she adored. Only Emma truly wasn't thinking—her mind was solely consumed with her brother and his problems. As Emma stripped down to her bra and panties all she sought in that moment was a clear head—a break from her frantic thoughts.

The water was delicious—refreshingly cold as she plunged in. There was nothing better than swimming in the ocean—the weightlessness, the pull of the waves, the invigorating feel of salt water on her skin and the bliss of escape. Here, Emma knew, she was just a speck in the scheme of things, and the vastness of the ocean soothed her mind, her panic abating as her body tired.

She had swum a long way out.

The first fingers of fear tightened around her heart as Emma stared back at the grey beach, her legs moving as she attempted to tread water, and at that moment terror seized her. She could see rocks moving alongside her even though she was trying to stay still, and felt the very real force of a seemingly benign ocean as it rapidly pulled away her from the shore.

She was caught in a rip. A fast-moving channel of current that ran perpendicular to the beach. She knew not to fight it—knew she could never swim against it—but the foolhardiness of her actions caught up with her. The vastness of the ocean that had moments ago soothed her scared her now.

He didn't want to go back.

Even though he had spent only twelve hours away from the city, Zarios actually felt as if he had had a break. Walking along the beach, the sun just starting to appear on the horizon—it was bliss to have the place to himself.

Last night had been nice, watching his father and Eric talking, and for once he had been able to relax and enjoy a pleasant evening without worrying about Miranda, about work, or the board's decision.

He was almost tempted to accept Lydia's offer to stay the entire weekend—to cancel his other engagements and to just get off the treadmill for a little while.

Except he couldn't.

It seemed everyone wanted a piece of him these days—everyone demanded their pound of flesh. It wouldn't even enter their heads that he really *needed* a weekend off—naturally they'd assume the worst.

That Zarios D'Amilo was boiling towards yet another scandal.

Oh, his father was upset—furious, in fact, that things hadn't worked out with Miranda, that another teary story would no doubt hit the magazines in a week or so, at a time when the D'Amilo name could least afford it. Zarios knew he had *tried* to make it work with her, but her behaviour had been becoming more and more bizarre. With each passing week she became more possessive, more demanding, till nothing bar a proposal of marriage would convince Miranda that he wasn't cheating on her. And though it might have soothed Miranda and might have appeased his father and their fellow directors, Zarios had refused to be pushed.

Once again, he hated how he had been judged.

Despite the scathing words that were written about him, despite his heartbreak reputation, he actually *loved* women—loved the rush that came at the beginning of a romance, that moment when he actually believed she might be the one who was different. Zarios went into every breathtaking relationship wishing over and over that this time he'd found her—that this time he'd met the one.

Picking up a stone, Zarios skimmed it out to the water.

The one!

'*Hah!*' He shouted out the word as he skimmed another stone.

There was no such thing as *the one*! He picked up a

handful, skimming them angrily now. Take Emma, for example. Had his father not warned him about her problem with money? Had he not seen it with his own eyes and heard it directly from Jake?

Well, she might have had him convinced for a while, but not for long, Zarios thought savagely. Never for long. Over and over he was proved right: women wanted only one thing—well, two if he was being accurate. And the second he was happy to provide for free!

He refused to be as blind as his father—a man who still loved the woman who had shamed him, who had walked out on her husband and child without a backward glance.

A woman who wanted to creep her way back now that his father was ill and about to retire... Well, she'd have to get past Zarios first. From his shorts he pulled out a letter, read again the needy words he had intercepted, then wrapped it in a stone and tossed it out to the ocean.

She was too late!

Thirty years too late. And if his father couldn't see that, then he was a fool.

For a moment he thought he was seeing things. Squinting out into the grey pre-dawn ocean, he saw a flash of something white. His heart stilled in his mouth as he saw it was a hand, and realised with dread that someone out there was in trouble.

His first instinct was to dive in, but Zarios fought it. The person was a long way out, and a clear head was what was needed here. Behind him was the lifeguard's shed, but he found it was locked. Soon he knew the first surfers would be coming, but for now it was down to him alone.

He was running before his plan had actually formulated in his mind. Already he was acting on it, running the length of the beach, scanning the slippery low rocks ahead, while whipping his head around every few seconds to the water, making sure he didn't lose sight of the swimmer.

The panic that had gripped him when he had realised it was a person out there in trouble had abated now. Zarios was running on pure adrenaline, focussing just as he did at work, only on the task in hand and not upon the stakes. It was a formula that had served him well.

Don't slip.

He told himself that as he reached the rocks. Just get to the mid-section.

She was still treading water.

She.

He pushed that thought aside as he navigated the sludge and seaweed, dragging in two large lungfuls of air as he calculated the distance and realised he was as close on land as he could get. Aware of the rocks, he lowered himself rather than dived in, kicking off with a powerful front crawl, looking up every now and then, keeping his eye on his target, feeling the power of the water beneath the relatively calm surface as he neared her.

Just like that she was gone.

A glimmer of fear crept in then—a first glimpse that he was too late. A frantic, urgent second of negotiation cluttered his mind. If he'd just run faster, swum quicker…if he dived under now… And then she resurfaced, blue eyes frantic, mouth open, arms flailing. For the first time in his life Zarios tasted pure, unadulterated fear. It seized him as if someone had touched his insides: this fury, this panic at what had nearly been lost.

What still could be lost.

He grabbed her, pulled her into the crook of his arm and lay on his back. Then with every ounce of strength he could muster he kicked and propelled his body back towards the rocks, swimming across the rip. Someone must have been really looking out for her, because just when his body was tiring a surfer, who must have seen the action from the beach, was there, helping her onto his board. The two men worked in silent unison to bring her to the shore, where she knelt in the shallows, coughing and retching and just so very, *very* lucky.

'*Stupido!*' He was beyond furious. Between dragging in lungfuls of air and coughing out half the ocean, still he managed to loudly point out first in rapid Italian and then in English what a fool she had been. Whatever language he spoke, the message was blatantly clear. '*Voi idiota stupido!* Swimming alone…'

Emma was kneeling in damp sand, coughing, shivering, too terrified to be grateful—too shaken to yet relish being alive. Instead of filling her hungry lungs she could only manage tiny shallow breaths. The panic that had gripped her in the ocean was nothing compared to her realisation of the fragility of existence. Of the thoughtless action that had nearly cost her life.

'Okay, mate…' Surfer boy must have seen it all before, because, though breathless himself, he was incredibly calm. 'She knows she made a mistake. You did the right thing, letting the rip carry you,' the boy reassured her as Zarios stood there silently fuming. 'You can't swim against it.'

Her breathing was slowing down now, delicious

oxygen creeping into every exhausted cell. Each and every breath was like a refreshing glass of lemonade, and she relished each one.

A little posse had formed—mainly lean, bronzed surfer-types, and an elderly woman who was walking her dog, all standing around her as she shivered in her bra and panties and in her own misery. A blanket was produced from the surf shed, and Emma was grateful for its heavy, musty warmth as it was wrapped around her shoulders.

'Did you take in a lot of water?' the surfer asked.

'No! I was just tiring. I'm fine now…'

'Maybe we should get you looked at?'

Emma shook her head. 'I just want to go home.'

She remembered to thank him, although Zarios actually remembered first, shaking his hand and then wrapping an arm around Emma's shoulders before leading her up the stony path to her parents' house. He even smiled and thanked the elderly lady when she rushed up, having retrieved Emma's clothes.

'Don't tell Mum…' Her teeth were chattering so violently she could hardly get the words out. 'I don't want to ruin the weekend.'

'You nearly took care of that…' He stopped himself from ramming home the inevitable point. 'Let's just hope they're not up yet…' His voice faded again.

Despite the early hour the marquee was already being taken down. Lydia was trilling her orders, anxious to get the place in shape before the champagne breakfast.

'What about in here…?' He pushed open the doors of the summerhouse, a pretty white room where her mother read and her father escaped. Leading her to a daybed, he sat her down, then set about locating a towel, taking the musty blanket from her shoulders and wrapping her in its soft warmth. 'We'll get you dry, and then you can get dressed and back to the house…she won't know.'

'You won't tell her?'

'On one condition.' He gripped her upper arms, his face stern and serious. 'You have to promise me that you will never do anything like that again.'

'I won't.'

'*Christo*, Emma…' His eyes burnt into hers, anger creeping back in. 'What possessed you?' He was drenched, his black hair almost blue, droplets of water still on his wide shoulders.

'I don't know…' She couldn't give a sensible reason. She'd grown up by the beach—knew the rules. Knew, knew, *knew*… 'I just wanted to clear my head. I'm just worried…'

'About what?'

She wanted to tell him so badly. In fact, she almost did, but even as she opened her mouth, she shook her head. Jake's gambling and the filthy, complicated mess he had created were just too big and scary to face, let alone share.

'I can't say.'

'You could.'

'I can't.'

'Okay, don't worry about it now…' His hands were stroking her through the towel, moving to her back, drying her off, then moving down to her legs. The floor was littered with sand. 'Let's get you dressed and inside.'

And then it *really* seemed to hit him. Zarios paused mid-stroke, bemused eyes looking up to hers.

'You could have died!'

Oh, there was no better warmth than his arms. Fiercely, he had pulled her from the daybed into his embrace, and kneeling he held her, held her, *held her*, as if checking that she was still there. And, Emma thought, being held was so much better than being told off—just feeling his heartbeat in her ear, his warmth imbuing her. For a full five minutes he held her, and whether it was adrenaline that propelled them, or just the sheer exhilaration of finding out just how sweet and precious life was, it felt entirely right that he kissed her.

It was the most thorough, expert and welcome kiss of her life. His mouth claimed hers, pressing hard into her shivering one, warming her as his body scooped her in. Kneeling, facing her, he devoured her with his mouth, kissing her harder and harder as though he still had to prove that she was really there, pausing for a second and then possessing her mouth again.

Just absolutely the best a kiss could be. Like a balm to her wounds. The horror that had consumed her simply faded. The soft stroke of his tongue, his taut body against hers, obliterated everything.

No kiss had ever moved her like this. She had thought last night's effort wonderful, but it had only skimmed the surface of what his mouth could do. His touch seemed to flick a trigger, unleashing in her such *want*. He was pushing down the straps of her bra, his mouth still pressing on hers, his rough and unshaven and utterly delicious jaw rasping her cheek. His skilled fingers impatiently unhooked her bra and tossed it aside. Her frozen and exhausted body was warming and waking beneath hands that massaged her full breasts as still he kissed her.

'I thought I'd lost you when you went under...'

He was talking as if he loved her, and her head was spinning with his words. He spoke as if they were, as if they had once been lovers. The world was spinning in a strange fast-forward, in recognition of some future time. Everything aligned as she knew, without it being said, that they were going to make love. The passion, the emotion that ripped through them, was inexplicable, almost, but utterly, utterly right. Kneeling still, they pressed so hard into each other it hurt—a hurt that reminded her she was alive!

As he kissed her cheeks, her ears, her eyelashes, and gently tugged at her panties, Emma remembered that she had nearly died. And nearly dying was a very, very good reason to start living, she told herself, as both of them stood just long enough to dispose of their few pieces of clothing.

And *this* was living!

She'd expected the frenzy to continue, but Zarios slowed things down. As they sank to their knees he rested on his heels, devouring every inch of her with hungry eyes, one single finger tracing the length of her body. She quivered under his scrutiny. Pathetically grateful she'd taken her panties off when she'd had a spray tan, Emma was agog with terror as she watched him harden to his full, impressive length. Her stomach curled inside as his fingers moved down and slowly stroked her damp blonde curls.

'All night I thought of you.' His knees parted hers, the dark hair on his legs scratching against her thighs, pushing them apart until he exposed her. He began to stroke her slowly.

Unable to stop herself, Emma admitted the same. 'I thought of you, too.'

She was having trouble breathing for entirely different reasons now.

'I thought of this.' He slid a finger inside her, the nub of his thumb working her clitoris. 'And then I thought of this…' He lowered his head and suckled on her nipple, the rhythmic sucking matching his handiwork.

Her head arched back as he worked her, and in a moment of weakness again she admitted the same. 'I thought of this, too.'

He was huge—worryingly so, excitingly so. Her head was back down, watching as her fingers instinctively reached for him as if they belonged to someone else. She began to stroke him in the same slow motion with which he was stroking her. She could see his mouth still suckling her breast, but she gazed down beyond it, one greedy finger taking the silver pearl of moisture from his tip and massaging it into the soft velvety skin that belied the strength beneath.

'*Attente!*' His voice was thick, the words spoken between greedy mouthfuls. 'Be careful.'

And then he looked up, warning her, offering her an out. But her voice, when it came, was absolutely sure. 'I don't *want* to be careful!'

It was all the confirmation he needed to go on, and, oh, the bliss as he guided her onto the daybed. She braced herself for his weight, but it never came, his fingers instead working their magic, sliding deep inside her as his erection hovered at her entrance. She was a frenzy of sensation, a bleating mess of indecision, wanting him to go on, but wanting him to come in. She could hear the sounds of her own moisture as he massaged her deeply, as he made sure beyond doubt that her tight space was oiled and ready to accommodate him. And thank heavens he did, because even with his lavish attention, even with a body that was cooing and aching to be filled, she felt a sudden pain when he entered, a delicious hurt as he filled her. The heat was building as he pushed so hard inside her, so deep within her, she could feel the bruise of her cervix.

She was coming, biting his salty chest, wrapping her calves around his muscular back. Still he bucked inside her, the throb of her orgasm gripping him, but it didn't match his strength because he pushed her on.

'Zarios...' She wanted him to stop, was almost scared that he might continue. Her twitching body was surely spent, but still she could feel him swell further, feel the more urgent, reckless staccato rhythm of his thrust, and she was coming again, her orgasm more intense than she could have ever dared to imagine it might be. Her hands were two balled fists of tension on his back. Unfurling her fingers was an impossible task as every muscle in her body twitched in spasm as she received him, felt a shudder of tension rip through him, and then the warm melt of him on her.

And then he kissed her.

His tongue was strangely cold as his lazy kiss brought her round, welcoming her back to a world that was brighter, and somehow very different.

'If I swim out again will you rescue me?'

'That is not funny.'

'Well, *that* wasn't a very good deterrent.'

'I might not be here next time to save you...'

As he looked down at her Emma realised that his eyes, though they looked black, were actually the darkest deepest indigo, more purple than blue, and a colour she wanted to capture and recreate with her brush. Only, even with her artistic prowess, she wasn't sure she could do the colour justice.

'Although I would like to be there.'

And she knew he wasn't talking about swimming— knew, because at that moment they were so close words were hardly needed. A new language was forming, and their minds were meeting with the same force their bodies had and blending just as perfectly.

'I'd like you to be there.'

'Let's get you back to the house.' He held her tighter as he spoke. 'This weekend cannot be about us. I want your father to enjoy his celebration.' He kissed her very slowly. 'Emma, this is big.'

A rather facetious comment was on the tip of her tongue, given the length of him on her thigh, but Emma restrained herself. Her mind was simply being kind, using humour to deflect the seriousness of his words for a moment. What they had just found was monumental.

'I know.'

There was nothing to joke about.

'We need to be very sure, and we need to get our heads around things ourselves before we share this with our families.'

Oh, he was right. If there was even a hint of romance today, the whole dynamics of the weekend would shift.

They had to get used to things first, before they revealed their feelings to the world.

There wasn't a flicker of question or doubt in her eyes as she stared back at him.

For that moment at least, she absolutely trusted him.

'There you are!' Lydia smiled when, a considerable time later, a rather bedraggled Emma appeared. 'We were about to send out a search party.'

'I was enjoying a walk.'

'And the water!' Lydia frowned at the knot of wet hair trailing down her back.

Given that it was now after eight Emma could be a touch honest. 'I had a swim—I couldn't resist.' Emma flushed, her heart thumping as, not for the first time, she realised just how disastrous the consequences might have been had Zarios not saved her. Thankfully Lydia was too wrapped up in preparing for the champagne breakfast to question her further. 'Do you need me to do anything, Mum?'

'Get changed, darling!' Lydia scolded, pulling out of the fridge the vast bowl of Strawberries Romanof that Emma had yesterday painstakingly prepared for the occasion without comment, then twittering with delight as she pulled back the cloth on the basket of rolls and pastries that had thankfully been delivered.

'He's gone way over the top, as always...' Lydia tutted at the contents. 'But then, that's Jake!'

The shower was bliss—warm water washing away the salt, her body burning still from Zarios's attention. Massaging conditioner into her hair, Emma closed her eyes and revelled in the sheer wonder of being alive, every nerve in her body tingling as she recalled his hands and mouth on her. Her heart was fluttering with excitement, and she cradled her knowledge like a treasured gift—scarcely able to comprehend that in just a few short hours everything had changed.

She dressed in pale khaki shorts and a white cotton halter neck, quickly blowdrying her hair and then tying it back in a loose ponytail, before adding just a little make-up. She joined her family and the D'Amilos out on the decking. Today was more intimate—just immediate family, which Rocco practically was, and of course Zarios.

He smiled as she entered, just a brief smile, but it confirmed every last thing she was feeling.

There was an exhilaration about her that perhaps had something to do with surviving a near death experience, or perhaps just the sheer pleasure of being with her family, all combined with the giddy recall of Zarios's lovemaking. For Emma it truly was the sweetest time, every second relished as she sipped on Bucks Fizz and listened to her father's laughter, saw her mother's face flushed and pretty with the relief that the her beloved Eric's birthday had gone so well. He was opening his gifts, smiling at the slippers, the tankards, at an expensive pair of binoculars for his beloved birdwatching, and then frowning at Rocco's gift.

'A phrasebook?'

'For when you come to visit me at my home in Rome.' Rocco waved away Eric's protests as he opened a travel itinerary along with two first class tickets. 'When Bella left—when I was on my own—every week you rang me, every week there was a letter, and every time I came back to Australia to check on my business here not once did I sleep in a hotel. You, my friends, were always there. Now it is time for you to eat at my table—for you, Eric, to take your wife to what is surely the most beautiful city in the world,' Rocco finished, wiping tears from his eyes as he told the couple the true value of their friendship.

Well, nothing was going to top that!

'Here, Dad.' Emma found she was biting on her lips as she handed her father her gift. An oil painting, it was of the beach scene from their house at late afternoon. Normally in her paintings Emma always left faces blank, so the people who bought her pieces were able to place themselves in the image—it was the signature mark of her work. Except in this one, amongst the families and children playing on the beach, unmistakably there were her parents, smiling and relaxed as they walked hand in hand along the beach they had loved for so long.

It had taken her days to paint.

But it had been weeks of thought that had drained her.

'It's lovely, darling.' Eric gave her a suitable smile as he studied her work for, oh, around ten seconds, before kissing her cheek.

'You and Mum are there…' Emma pointed to the figures in the scene.

He pulled on his glasses and peered more closely. 'So we are!' Eric beamed, then took his glasses off and kissed her on the cheek again. 'Thank you, darling.'

He put the painting down on the floor beside the mountain of other presents, then peeled open the gift Jake and Beth had bought, crowing in delight at a bottle of champagne Emma could have sworn she'd given them as a gift when the twins were born, and holding up the two department store champagne glasses that accompanied the bottle as if they were made of the finest crystal.

'That's for you two to share,' Jake said, and smiled, 'when the party's over. Happy birthday, Dad!'

Emma found she was biting hard into her lip as her mother oohed and ahed, kissing Jake and telling him he was so thoughtful. Her fingers were clenched, and in an effort not to say anything, not to spoil things, Emma actually sat on her hands, telling herself she was being unreasonable. Her father *had* been delighted with her present. She was just being sensitive, that was all, because Rocco was nodding at the lovely champagne and Zarios was busy with his mobile phone. She was surely just being childish. But was she the only one who could see the glaring disparity between how she and Jake were treated? Blinking back sudden pathetic tears, Emma was glad of the diversion of her own phone bleeping. Picking it up from the table, she frowned slightly when she saw that she had a message from Zarios.

Don't sulk!

She suppressed a smile as she texted back.

Do you blame me?

As she hit 'send', the sound of his phone bleeping at the opposite end of the table sent a fizz of excitement through her—especially when she saw that he was texting again.

I liked it.

She was about to text back her thanks, but she had another incoming message.

I want you.

Two spots of colour burnt on her cheeks as her phone bleeped again, and Zarios told her exactly how *much* he wanted her. She was blushing like an eighteen-year-old—*felt* like an eighteen-year-old as her mother's frown scolded her for spending so long on her phone.

'Could you get some more orange juice, Emma?'

'Of course.'

She fled to the kitchen, embarrassed yet exhilarated, as jumpy as a cat. She trembled as she pulled open the door of the fridge. It wasn't just that he was sexy—though he was, Emma thought, gulping icy air from the fridge—it was that smile, that lazy smile that just made the world pause, and the intensity of his eyes when they held hers.

And instinctively he had known how much her father's dismissal of her work, however unwitting, had hurt her.

Never had a man read her more skilfully.

It was as if he'd versed himself in her thoughts—like an extension to her mind.

He *got* it!

Got the crazy make-up of her family and the fact that

they could make her smile, make her laugh, even as they drove her round the bend.

'Need a hand?'

He didn't wait for an answer. His hot palm was between her legs, running lazily the length of her thigh, and she rested her head on the freezer door to steady herself, simultaneously revelling in his touch and tensing at the thought of anyone walking in.

'Zarios…' She turned to face him, to warn him off with a brittle expression, to tell him this was neither the time nor the place—but he'd beaten her to it. He was smiling down at her, pulling out cartons from the fridge and feigning such utter innocence that if her thighs hadn't been on fire she'd have sworn she'd imagined the whole thing.

Zarios had been confused by her parents' reaction to the painting—had been confused by the gift as well. From the way Lydia had spoken, and from the information he had gleaned over the years, he had assumed Emma's hobby had simply been indulged by Lydia and Eric.

But with one glance he'd seen her talent.

A real talent that should be nurtured and applauded, not tossed amongst a pile.

He was lying, and they both knew it, when he tried to say the right thing. 'I know how it looked out there,' Zarios said as he picked up some jugs from the bench, 'but they *are* proud of you!'

'I think you're talking to the wrong sibling.' She snipped open the juice and poured it into the jugs. 'They're proud of the one with the *real* job and the fancy car—the one who gives them grandchildren…'

'You're incredibly talented.'

'That doesn't always sell paintings!' She hadn't meant to say anything, but the financial pressure Jake had heaped on her fledgling business was just too much to bear, and unwittingly, just as her mother did when stressed, Emma put down the carton and massaged her temples for a moment.

'Business not going too well?'

'Just a few money worries at the moment; it will pick up,' she said, doing just that to the juice. But his hands caught hers, making them let go of their contents.

'Tomorrow?' Zarios said, stunned by the comfort saying that single word gave him.

'Tomorrow,' she agreed, taking a deep breath, and then another rapid one, as he deeply kissed the nape of her neck. He kissed it so hard that when she fled to the loo moments later she could see the bruise he had left, which had her pulling out her ponytail and arranging her hair to hide it. She had been angry with him at the time, and yet was surprisingly grateful later.

Grateful, because when everyone had gone, when the chopper had long since lifted into the sky, and her parents had read through the cards for the hundredth time and all that was left was the tidying up, it was almost impossible to fathom what had taken place.

She checked her phone for the hundredth time, willing a text to appear, telling herself it didn't matter that there wasn't one—he was at a christening; he'd told her he'd speak to her tomorrow…

Later, having undressed for bed, exhausted, she brushed her teeth, and then, lifting her hair, saw again the smudge of purple bruise. She shivered, running her fingers over the only tangible evidence of what had taken place. Emma clutched the memory of it to her like a hot water bottle as she curled up in the same bed Zarios had slept in last night, slid under the weighty warmth of a duvet that still held his scent and let memories caress her exhausted body.

Remembered the bliss of being in his arms.

Willed sleep to come so that soon she could greet the morning.

CHAPTER FOUR

'COME with us, darling,' Lydia said again, as Emma read the morning paper. 'We're going to drive along the coast and have a long, lazy lunch…'

'I really can't, Mum.' Emma shook her head. 'I haven't been at the gallery since Thursday.'

'Surely one more day off won't hurt?' Lydia pushed.

Oh, but it would. A buyer had been in twice the previous week, looking at her paintings, and Emma knew that a closed sign on her shop too many days in a row would soon temper his interest. And then there was Jake to deal with.

She jumped with nervous excitement as her phone shrilled, dismayed and panicked to find that it was just Jake—wanting to know her answer, wanting to know what time she was getting away so that they could talk.

'I need to be at the shop.' Emma filled her cup from the pot and added sugar. 'Anyway…' she smiled as her dad walked in and pinched Lydia's bottom '…you two don't need me sitting in the back seat spoiling your fun. You've got a trip to Rome to plan!'

'I can't believe Rocco was so generous!' Lydia clapped her hands in delight at the prospect. 'I just can't believe he did that.'

'I can...' Eric slathered butter on his toast. 'He's always wanted to show us his home town, and I think, with his retirement coming up and everything...' he paused for a pensive moment '...he's probably wondering how he'll fill his time.'

'I know how *I'd* fill it!' Lydia shook her head in wonder. 'He should be off on a cruise. The women would be lining up for him, with his pots of money...and he's a nice man, too,' Lydia added, more as an afterthought.

'You're incorrigible!' Eric laughed, but his expression was serious. 'He's a *very* nice man who happens to still be in love with his ex-wife.'

'Then he needs to get over her!' Lydia said, unmoved. 'You know I love you, Eric, but I wouldn't wait thirty years.'

'She wouldn't wait thirty minutes!' Eric winked at his daughter, peeling off the front and sports pages of the newspaper, as he always did. 'Have you had a good weekend, darling?'

'I had a great time,' Emma enthused. 'Everyone did!'

'You're sure?' Lydia checked. 'Did you hear anyone actually *say* that?'

'Everyone had a ball...' Emma's voice trailed off as she turned the page, everything freezing as Zarios's face suddenly stared out at her from the newspaper. He wasn't alone.

He was with Miranda.

The regular Monday gossip column, telling what had happened with the rich and famous over the weekend, was causing more than a vague stir of interest as Emma read the words below the photo.

The rumoured break-up of drop-dead gorgeous financier Zarios D'Amilo and his model girlfriend Miranda Deloware (pictured yesterday, wearing an exquisite Kovlosky gown), seems to be just that: a rumour.

Appearing together at the christening of Elizabeth Hamilton (see p42) there was no mistaking that they were very much a couple. A source close to the pair hinted there might soon be the sound of wedding bells.

Sorry, gals…it would appear Zarios is very much spoken for.

'I thought as much…' Lydia tutted as she peered over Emma's shoulder. 'Any woman would be mad to get involved with him.'

'That's not what you said on Saturday.'

'I hadn't spoken properly to Rocco then. Zarios is the incorrigible one! He's got the morals of an alley cat, apparently; he'll say anything to get a woman into bed. Really, I can see why Rocco's hesitant to just hand everything over to him.' She stabbed at his image in the paper. 'Zarios doesn't know the meaning of the word *commitment.*'

Somehow Emma managed to be normal.

Somehow she managed to kiss her parents goodbye and thank them for a wonderful weekend as they headed off for their drive along the coast.

She wasn't even angry as she clipped on her seatbelt and headed for her own long drive home, still hoping that he'd ring, that her phone would bleep and it would be Zarios, offering some sort of an explanation.

Pulling up at her flat, Emma felt her heart leap as she

saw him standing at her door, glad—so glad—that she hadn't rung and blasted him with accusations.

He gave a very thin half-smile of acknowledgement as she parked her car, then walked towards him, and Emma felt her heart sink at the grim expression on his face.

'Hi.' Refusing to be needy or jealous, refusing to let him know she'd even *seen* the newspaper, Emma let him into the hallway then up the steep steps towards her flat. She certainly wasn't going to make this easy for him—if he was still with Miranda then he could tell her so without assistance!

'I've been waiting for you…' He couldn't meet her eyes; he followed her through to the kitchen. 'May I?' He gestured to the sink and Emma frowned as he poured himself a glass of water and downed it in one gulp. For someone who had had so much practice in breaking women's hearts, he sure looked nervous. 'As I said, I've been waiting for you.'

'Well, I'm here now!' Emma kept smiling, *deliberately* kept smiling, even though her heart was shrivelling. Just yesterday she'd been in his arms. Little more than twenty-four hours ago she'd been foolish enough to glimpse a future with Zarios in it—and now she knew, just knew, he was about to break her heart.

What an idiot she was to believe him.

What a blind, trusting fool.

'Your brother asked me to come…'

'My brother?' Emma frowned. What on earth did Jake have to do with all this? Unless he'd been asking Zarios for money… Emma's blood chilled at the very thought.

'He's at the hospital…' Zarios ran a tongue over very

pale lips. 'We thought it better that I came and told you rather than the police…'

'The police…' Tiny needles prickled at her scalp, along her arms. Her eyes shot to his, seeing the very real anguish there. 'What's he done?' Frantic images dotted her mind. Oh, she'd known Jake was worried—in deep trouble, perhaps—but from the serious note in Zarios's voice, from the grey tinge to his skin and his reticence, Emma knew that this was serious. 'What's happened to Jake?'

'It's not Jake.'

Her hand flew to her mouth as she thought of Beth, the twins… 'What the hell has he done?'

'It isn't Jake, Emma…' Zarios swallowed hard. 'It's your parents.'

'My parents?' She shook her head. Nothing he was saying was making sense. 'What are you talking about? I just left them.'

'There was an accident on the beach road…'

She was already turning for the door, desperate to get to them, only Zarios was pulling her back.

And she knew why—knew as he pulled her into his chest what was coming next. Only she didn't want to hear it. Struggling like a frantic cat in his grasp, she was desperate to get away, to flee, to run, rather than be held and face the truth.

'Emma, they were killed outright.'

CHAPTER FIVE

His arms were the only thing that stopped her falling as everything in her world went black.

In the horrible shrinking vortex which she'd entered, for a moment there was nothing. No sound, no thought, no gravity. Just a spinning sensation of doom that coated each cell in its rapid black welcome, then expelled her to another side—a side where, no matter how she pleaded and wept to go back, there was no escape.

On the most horrific day of her life he was there beside her, this strong pillar of support. In fact, Emma was so bewildered that she didn't even realise till much later how much she must have leant on him that day.

And that evening, too.

She had let him drive her back to her parents' home and there lead her to her bed, where she had woken just that morning when everything had been so normal. He had sat on the chair beside her whilst she had drifted in the twilight zone between rest and sleep to a place of vague awareness, and somewhere between darkness and dawn she remembered.

'Miranda…'

'Shhh…' The loose lips of a liar might once have

soothed her, but she was beyond comfort now, beyond pain—beyond anything, really.

'Are you two back together?'

'We'll talk in the morning.'

'Are you back together?'

The endless silence before he spoke was louder than his words.

'Emma, it's complicated....'

'Yes or no?'

There was the longest pause. 'Yes.'

Which still didn't answer her question. It was unfathomable to her that after the most breathtaking lovemaking, after all that had been said, he could within a matter of hours simply walk away.

'Is she pregnant?' It was an arrogant question, but it was all she could think of, all that could rationalise such a rapid demise.

'No.' Zarios looked her in the eyes and lied. Lied because they *had* to be over. Lied because he wouldn't do it to his child—could never let it be said, even to himself, that it was the only reason he was with its mother.

'Miranda and I have been together a long time— four months,' Zarios added. And Emma suddenly felt as if her mother was in the room with her, recalling the sun-drenched evening and how they had laughed. The perfect answer was there for the taking, but she chose not to use it. 'Emma, what happened that morning…'

He closed his eyes; she could see his face screwed up in concentration as he tried to find the words, but rather than wait for his paltry summing up, she found words for him.

'Was just a bit of fun.'

He frowned before he opened his eyes again. Clearly her response was the last thing he'd been expecting, but Emma was hurting so badly that there was plenty to go around, so instead of humiliating herself, instead of letting him think she'd once wanted him, she told him otherwise. She was more than willing to grate off a piece of her raw bruised heart and let him sample the pain—let him take a sip of the humiliation he'd force-fed her.

'Emma, you know that's not the case.'

The acrid bitter taste of humiliation was choking her. She had lost not just her parents that day, but the man she'd glimpsed loving, too.

'Oh, come on, Zarios, my mother would never have forgiven me if I hadn't at least attempted to flirt with you.' She stared through the darkness towards him. 'The great Zarios D'Amilo, coming to my house for a party. My business almost in tatters. It would have been almost criminally irresponsible for me not to at least *try*…' And there it was, the tiniest swallow in his olive throat that told her that maybe, just maybe, he believed her. It was enough to make her go on. 'So you went back to Miranda—oh, well, you can't blame a girl for trying. Anyway, you know how the saying goes—rich men are like buses; if you miss one, there will be two more following shortly behind.'

Silence hissed in the air. Emma knew she had gone too far, but it was too late to attempt retrieval, and right now she simply didn't care.

'Just leave, Zarios.'

'You shouldn't be on your own.'

'Then I'll ring someone I want to have here.'

'Well—' his voice was crisp and businesslike, but the

contempt in his eyes would surely stay with her for ever '—I'm glad we both understand each other.'

'Me, too.'

It was Zarios who had the final word.

'I wouldn't waste your time on your artwork, Emma. After your performance in the summerhouse you should try your hand at acting. For a minute there I actually believed you were different.'

CHAPTER SIX

PRIVATELY Emma had often wondered how Jake would cope in a real crisis—the answer had surprised her.

He had dealt with everything—and not just the practical—had offered endless support as Emma struggled just to function. He had dealt with the rapid sale of her parents' house when, two days after the funeral, a generous offer had come up to buy it, furnishings and all. And Jake had offered wise counsel when, on a particularly unbearable night, she'd confided to him what had happened with Zarios.

'You're best out of it, Em…' He had held her hand and said all the right things. 'Whatever he's got going on with Miranda is just to keep the board of directors happy—it will be over in a few weeks.'

And he had been right.

Two weeks before the board's decision and Zarios was again in the newspapers—but for all the wrong reasons.

She'd read about him—unable to help herself—with a morbid curiosity, scanning the magazines and newspapers.

D'Amilo Financiers shareholders were bracing themselves for the announcement, its share price hovering as the financial world held its collective breath and awaited details on the company's new direction. For a while Zarios had managed to behave. Emma had winced at every photo of him walking hand in hand with Miranda, hopping on a plane and joining her in Brazil on a photo-shoot. His spin doctors had been working overtime, almost managing to convince the world that Zarios D'Amilo had changed—that this leopard now wore different spots.

Till last week.

No comment had been offered from Camp Zarios when Miranda had been dumped at the eleventh hour, just two weeks short of his father's retirement. The papers were ablaze with the scandal, the share price had tumbled, and even the gossip magazines wavered in their dogged devotion to Zarios.

After all, Emma thought, her lips curling in distaste as she'd read on, what reputable magazine could favourably report on a man who would end a relationship when he found out Miranda was unable to bear children?

Zarios, as Miranda had tearfully revealed to the enthralled media, having sold her story for a record sum, had wanted a child, an heir, and had refused to commit to marriage until she became pregnant. Tests had recently revealed that she was infertile, and there were photos of the two of them coming out of the specialist fertility department at a top Melbourne hospital—Zarios looking boot-faced, Miranda in floods of tears.

And, Emma had noticed with loathing, he wasn't even holding her hand.

Jake had been right—she *was* best out of it. And then suddenly her brother had changed his mind.

Arriving at her door a couple of nights ago, grey and ashen, suddenly Jake had insisted that she went to Zarios for help.

Emma felt nauseous at the mere recollection of the desperate conversation she had shared with her brother that night.

'You *hit* Beth?' she had asked, appalled at her brother's confession.

'I pushed her…' Jake was as irritated as Emma was horrified. 'And she fell. I was just trying to get past and she was in the way. Look, Em…' in an attempt to soften her, Jake reverted to her childhood nickname '…how can I walk in now and tell Beth I've lost the house? She's already threatening to leave. Surely Zarios owes you after what he did to you? You can sweet-talk him into a loan.'

'He's not going to pay off your gambling debts.'

'Tell him it's for *you*! Tell him that your business is in trouble—tell him anything, just keep me out of it. He'd never agree for me. He knows our parents' house had been sold, that the money's practically in the bank—it's just till Mum and Dad's money comes through.'

'Even if he did give me a loan, which is highly un-likely, what are you going to tell Beth? How are you going to explain it in a couple of weeks' time, when you have to pay me back?'

'Things will be calmer then,' Jake said. 'If I tell her now, she'll walk. She'll take out a restraining order and I won't see the kids.'

'What if I go with you and speak to the bank? Maybe if you can sign a guarantee that the money's coming.'

'The guys I'm dealing aren't going to wait for the

bank to make up their mind, Em. I need…' Jake gulped as he told her the appalling figure—he needed nearly one million dollars by the close of business tomorrow. 'Every day that passes it goes up more…'

Those poor kids… Emma almost wept as she pictured Harriet's and Connor's innocent, trusting faces. Poor Beth, too. God alone knew what *she* must be putting up with.

What would her parents want her to do?

'I can't take this much longer, Emma.'

There was her answer. So now, with Jake's veiled threat still ringing in her ears, for the first time since her parents' funeral Emma dressed carefully.

But it took for ever.

Since their death it had felt as if her brain was working in slow motion. Her stomach was knotted in constant tension and the simplest decision took for ever to make: which shoes to wear, hair up or down, even whether to apply make-up—all required a mammoth effort, one she didn't want to make. And she'd never thought she would be making it for Zarios.

The putrid words of their last conversation still rang in her ears at times. She hated what she'd said to him, but hated what he'd done to her even more. She could see clearly how he'd used her that weekend—she'd been nothing more than a small diversion in an otherwise boring weekend. Emma had played with the big boys, she realised, and only had herself to blame for getting well and truly burnt.

And now she had to face him. Had to swallow her pride and ask the snake for help.

Which was easier said than done. His work life, as

Emma had found out when she had tried to contact him, was as capricious as his personal life—Rome one week, Singapore the next. He was flying from his office in Sydney down to Melbourne today, Emma had discovered on her third attempt to contact him, and surprisingly he'd agreed to meet her—or rather his secretary had arranged an appointment for 2:00 p.m. the following day, which had given her twenty-four hours to change her mind.

As if she had a choice.

She frowned at her dressing table as if it belonged to someone else, noticing that her hand was shaking as she stroked her make-up brush into powder. The two pink dots that appeared on her cheeks were just too much against her pale complexion and Emma wiped them off with a tissue, giving up on her face and grabbing her bag instead, clipping down the steep stairs of her flat. What the hell was the point of wearing make-up anyway? Nothing was going to disguise her humiliation—nothing was going to mask the shame of going to Zarios with a begging bowl in her hand.

'My appointment was at two.' Emma tried to keep the slightly desperate note from her voice. 'It's almost three now.'

The receptionist gave her a pussycat smile, which without words told Emma in no uncertain terms that she was more than capable of telling the time. 'Mr D'Amilo is an extremely busy man. As I've said, I'll inform you as soon as he's ready to see you.'

Not *that* busy!

Strolling through the lavish foyer, Zarios looked

completely refreshed and relaxed after his extended lunch. Maybe it had something to do with the company he was keeping.

A well-groomed brunette was beside him, hanging on his every word, laughing at whatever it was that Zarios had just said.

Emma had forgotten just how beautiful he really was. In the past few weeks, whenever her mind had drifted to him, or she'd read about his heartless, torrid break-up with Miranda, somehow her mind had managed to distort his image to almost devil-like proportions, marring his beauty perhaps to shield herself. But seeing him now, breathtakingly elegant in a charcoal-grey suit, his shirt gleaming white against his olive skin, there was no denying his beauty. He'd had his hair cut, those jet locks cropped closely to his head, which made him look more menacing and somehow more striking, if that were possible. Seeing him in the flesh even more than two months on had Emma's stomach curling—not at what she must now ask, but at what they had once shared.

When he spoke briefly to his receptionist, Emma was unclear whether she had let him know that his 2:00 p.m. appointment was waiting, because Zarios didn't even deign to give her a glance. Instead he headed towards the lifts and disappeared, leaving Emma more intimidated than ever at the prospect of what lay ahead.

It was another ten minutes till she was directed to his floor.

And another half an hour spent sitting in another waiting room—albeit a lavish one.

The groomed brunette must be his personal assistant, Emma realised, when she brought her an extremely welcome glass of iced water and peered at her from her desk when she thought Emma wasn't looking. Emma bit her lip as she awaited her fate, and then, with just an hour till the office building closed, the intercom buzzed and the snooty brunette finally gave her a nod. She was shown through.

'You wanted to see me.' There was no small talk, no apology for the delay. He curtly gestured for her to take a seat, his face utterly unreadable as tentatively she nodded.

'Regarding?'

He certainly wasn't making this easy.

'It's difficult…' Emma attempted.

'Then let me help you. We slept together approximately two months ago, and now you urgently need to meet with me—I can hazard a guess—'

'No!' Emma interrupted. The arrow he had shot had missed its mark, skimming over her shoulder surely to be forgotten. Except a sound resonated, a small hollow summons to tell her that somewhere it had hit a mark. But with a determined, irritated shake of her head she ignored it. 'I got my period on the day of my parents' funeral. That's not the reason I called.' Only now did he frown. Only now did he seem curious as to why she might be here. 'I wanted to see you about the release of my parents' money.'

'Of course!' Zarios gave a tight smile. 'Silly me for assuming otherwise!'

Emma ran a dry tongue over even dryer lips, embarrassment stinging every pore at his implication, regretfully acknowledging that after their bitter parting he was right to think as he did. She forced herself to continue. 'The house has been sold…'

'I believe so.'

'The thing is…' She blew a breath skywards, but her fringe barely moved; it was plastered to her moist forehead. 'I need access to my share of the funds now.'

'Now?'

'Yes. Today.' She watched his eyebrows rise just a fraction.

'Can I ask why you need money so quickly?'

'No.' She choked the single word out, then, clearing her throat, said it more firmly. 'No. I'd rather not say, but as soon as the sale of the house goes through I will repay the money. It would just be a loan until then.'

'I can see that a lot of work has gone into your proposal!'

His sarcasm, though merited, wasn't exactly helping. 'I realise it can't look good, me just walking in and asking for money. But I have my reasons, and the inheritance—'

'I can't help you.' He interrupted her, shaking his head.

'Please.' She hated that she was reduced to begging, but she had no choice. 'Zarios, please. You're the only person who has access to that type of funds…'

'Not quite…' He flashed a mirthless smile. 'Have you ever heard of banks?' Tears pricked her eyes as he savagely continued. 'If you are so convinced it is just a short-term loan, that in two weeks you can repay, then you should have no trouble securing a bridging loan. Of course a bank would want to know where the money was going, why a twenty-five-year-old woman needs access to such a sum of money at such short notice. Have you even *tried* the banks?'

She tried to say no, but the word wouldn't come out. Emma settled instead for a tiny shake of her head.

'Then am I right in assuming that is because you couldn't suitably answer their questions?'

Oh, *how* he must be enjoying this, Emma thought, the tears in her eyes drying as she stared at him across the desk, their mutual contempt meeting in the middle.

'Anyway,' he continued when she didn't answer, still holding her stare, 'even if I wanted to help you I could not.' He gave a dismissive shrug. 'There's a potential conflict of interest. I have excused myself from the board in regard to the execution of your parents' estate.'

'That's not what I'm asking…'

'I know that!' Zarios sneered. 'You are playing on the fact that we *once* slept together.'

'No!' Emma quivered. 'I'm pleading to you as a friend of the family.'

'Did you approach my father with your request?' Zarios snapped his very good point out. 'Of course not!'

'You know,' he continued bitterly, 'he said I was over-reacting when I removed myself from having any dealings with your parents' estate.' He stood up, clearly ending the meeting. 'Clearly I was right to follow my instincts.'

'You'll get it back…' Tears were streaming down her cheeks unchecked now. The thought of telling Jake, the thought of him telling Beth, the horrible reality of it all was unbearably close now, making her desperate. But her tears didn't move him. If anything they just compounded his disdain. 'I'll sign anything—the day the exchange happens you'll get the money back…'

'If you'll excuse me?' He glanced at his watch and pressed a button on his phone. 'I'm running behind schedule.' He smiled as his secretary opened the door, gave her a sort of wide-eyed look that acknowledged yet another tearful woman was leaving the building, and asked if she could please arrange that it was done quietly. 'Could you show Ms Hayes to the lift, please?'

As easily as that he dismissed her. His cold eyes made it clear there would be no further discussion, and the distaste was evident in the set of his face as he held open the door.

And who could blame him for what he must be thinking? Emma thought as the lift plummeted downwards—her parents were barely cold in their grave and she wanted her hands on their money with no questions asked, if that could possibly be arranged!

Clearly it couldn't.

She could feel her phone vibrating in her bag, knew it was Jake. For a tiny second she was almost relieved. Relieved that she couldn't help him. Relieved that the problem was no longer hers...

But then she heard his voice.

'Maybe Beth will understand...' Emma attempted as she told him the hard news. 'Maybe it's time to come clean, Jake—time to lay it all out in the open...'

'It's not what Beth's going to say that I'm worried about.' She could hear the fear in her brother's voice. 'Oh, God, what have I done, Em?' He was sobbing so hard he could barely get the words out. 'I can't face this! What are they going to do to me? What if they turn on her, on the kids? I'd be better off out of it.'

She was half walking, half running through the foyer.

She could hear the desperation in his voice and knew she had to get to him and turned, wild-eyed, when the receptionist stopped her in her tracks.

'Mr D'Amilo will see you shortly.'

Emma briefly closed her eyes in frustration before answering. 'I've already seen Mr D'Amilo.' She gave a very short smile, tempted to add, *for all the good it did.* She turned her attention back to her brother, but the receptionist persisted.

'I'm aware of that. Mr D'Amilo has asked that you wait while he considers your proposal further. If you'd like to take a seat, he'll send for you in due course.'

She had no idea what game Zarios was playing—the only thing she was certain of was that it was a game! How she would have loved to ignore the command to sit. But Jake was still on the line—or rather, Emma thought, Jake was at the very end of the line.

'Just hold on, Jake.' She put the phone back up to her ear. 'Just calm down. I'll sort out something. I'll talk to Zarios again.'

Despite the air-conditioning, sweat was beading on his forehead. Zarios felt as if his tie was choking him. Loosening it, he pulled open the top button of his shirt and tried to kick his stalled brain into some sort of action.

In an attempt to make things work with Miranda he'd relegated all the good things that he had shared with Emma to the recesses of his mind—had ignored the wonderful parts in the short life of their relationship and focussed solely on the death of it. He had replayed Emma's finishing words like a mantra every time his mind had wandered in that dangerous direction. But even if he had discounted their lovemaking, their passion, long before today, no matter how he had tried he hadn't been able to discount *her*.

And now she was back.

From the second he'd heard she was trying to make contact Zarios had been bracing himself—warning himself not to overreact, that if she did tell him she was pregnant he would stay calm... Except she wasn't pregnant.

Opening his office drawer for the first time that week, he pulled out the hand-sized teddy bear, with its smiling face and black button eyes, and managed to really look at it. He remembered the mawkish pride that had filled him when he'd paid for the little thing and had looked forward to sharing it with Miranda.

Just the thought of Miranda made his jaw clench.

The slurs, the innuendoes, the filth that had been reported this past week should have had him shouting the truth from the rooftops—should have propelled him to come out of his corner fighting. Except in the abyss of his pain the slights of the press had barely touched the sides.

Grief was the only thing that consumed him now.

A grief he couldn't understand and one he certainly couldn't explain—even to himself.

Resting his head in his hands, Zarios forced himself to breath evenly, to hold it together, to rise above it as he always did.

He had business to attend to.

And now, waiting downstairs, was the one woman who could possibly make his father believe that he had changed. Zarios's frozen brain was leaping into action now. He could even tell his father Emma was the *real* reason he had ended things with Miranda.

Stuffing the teddy back in the drawer, he slammed it shut, annoyed with himself for indulging in sentiment. The time for mourning was over.

Straightening his tie, he pressed on the intercom and told Jemima, his receptionist, to send her back in. After all…how could you mourn something that never even existed?

It was well after five before she was summoned. Way too late, Emma figured, for Zarios to do anything. The banks would have long since closed. Again the receptionist swiped her security tag for the lift and Emma headed to Zarios's floor. The only difference was that this time his snooty PA wasn't there to greet her. The sumptuous waiting area was empty, and Emma took a tentative seat, unsure what to do. She was also unsure what Zarios could possibly want with her now, so absolute had been his refusal to help.

She jumped slightly when his heavy office door opened and Zarios himself wordlessly gestured for her to come inside.

'You waited.'

He stood at the window, staring out at the darkening Melbourne sky that was thick with rain despite the summer month. Threatening droplets splashed onto the window and she knew that in a few moments, when he'd finished playing whatever his little game was, there was no doubt she'd be out there.

'I had no choice but to wait.'

'There are always choices.'

'Not always.' She took a seat uninvited, angry now. What choice had her parents had? What choice did *she* have now other than to sit and wait to see what the master had to say?

'You will have read about my break-up with Miranda?' He didn't turn to see her response; there was just a natural assumption that she had. 'My father and the board are less than impressed.'

As they should be, Emma thought, but didn't have the nerve to say it. Her voice was shaky when, after a moment, she found it. 'Is it true?' Emma swallowed. 'That you left her because she couldn't have your babies?'

'Why do you owe so much money?' Zarios countered, and when she didn't answer he gave a wry smile. 'We both have our own set of excuses, I am sure. When I first started working for my father it was a small company—building and refurbishing, here in Melbourne and in Rome. I found a property in Scotland—a castle that had the potential to be renovated into a top-class boutique hotel, ideal for weddings, that type of thing...'

Her head pounded with neuralgia. Why the hell was he telling her this? She didn't need a history lesson, she needed cash!

He must have sensed her impatience. 'Don't worry— I am as loath as you are to be in conversation. Believe me, this is not idle chatter!'

'Good.' She accepted the glass of water he poured, draining it in one gulp, not caring whether or not it was ladylike.

'For that to come to fruition we had to borrow, or bring investors on board. My father chose the latter option, and when the situation was repeated he brought in more investors. Ten years ago I was a year younger than you are now—twenty-four years old and still somewhat intimidated by father. The company was divided, with my father retaining a twenty-five percent stake, myself twenty-four. I strongly advised him to make his share twenty-six, mine twenty-five—are you still with me, Emma?' He must have seen her eyes glaze over, because he snapped her to rapid attention. 'Had he listened to me then, we would not be having this conversation now.'

'I can do the maths.' Emma gave a tight smile.

'Good—then you will know how important that two percent share is now, when D'Amilo Financials is worth billions. Once my father retires our directors want to rename it, and for my father's stake in the company to be spread between all the directors rather than passed to me—naturally, I am opposed.'

'What about your father?' Emma blinked. 'Surely it's up to him…?'

'He wants what is best for the future of the company, and on recent form he is not sure that is me. As he has said, whatever happens I am still a majority shareholder.' He registered her frown. 'My relationship with my father is not the same as the one you had with your parents. He is more a business partner to me than a parent.'

'What does this have to do with me?'

'My father wants to see me settled. He is unwell.'

The clipped tone of his voice told Emma he wasn't angling for sympathy, but no matter what she thought of the son, Emma cared about the father. 'What's wrong with him?' She watched Zarios's jaw stiffen, saw a flash of annoyance dart across his features at the invasive nature of her question. Finally he gave a brief, reluctant nod, before answering. 'He requires major heart surgery. His colleagues do not know—I would prefer that it stays that way.'

'Of course,' Emma responded. 'I'm very sorry to hear that.'

He neither wanted nor acknowledged her comment. Instead he moved swiftly on. 'This is why he is retiring so quickly. He was going to tell your parents about the surgery after your father's birthday. Given the seriousness of the matter, he is busy getting his affairs in order. He made it clear that if I toned down my behaviour, if I gave him reason to believe that I had changed, he would go against the rest of the board and transfer his stake to me. Miranda and I breaking up has almost put paid to that. However—' he gave a wan smile '—just when it seemed irretrievable a solution has appeared.' He gave Emma a black smile. 'He thinks the world of you.'

'He warned you *off* me!' Emma pointed out. 'I only wish you'd listened at the time.'

'He doesn't want me to hurt you, Emma!' His lips pouted and he blew her a mock kiss. 'Which is why we're getting engaged!'

'Please!'

'I've never made it official with a woman before…' He smiled at the novelty of his own treachery. 'It would go a long way to convincing him!'

'He'd never believe it.'

'You're too modest!' Zarios chided, his sardonic smile mocking her. 'Why, you're an excellent liar and a consummate actress, Emma! Personally, I'd *never* have taken you for a gold-digging whore!'

'Bastard!'

'Then we understand each other,' he drawled. 'You'll have no problem convincing him.'

'As if he's going to accept that we're suddenly together—' Emma shook her head. His proposal was too preposterous for words.

'Why wouldn't he?' Zarios interrupted. 'We will tell him the truth. We met up again after many years at your father's sixtieth birthday party and the attraction was immediate.'

Which *was* the truth, Emma conceded. But only so far!

'With all that has happened to you recently, it is no wonder things have moved so quickly. Of course it was hard, ending things with Miranda, but my feelings for you…' his eyes were black with malice '…were just impossible to ignore.'

'Why?' Emma blinked. 'Why does it matter to you so much? You're going to be rich either way…'

'Honour,' Zarios said. 'Look it up in the dictionary when you get home. You might learn something!'

'Honour amongst thieves, you mean!' Emma responded. 'You're asking me to lie to your own father, remember.'

'My father is too easily swayed by others—he has the Italian curse of worrying too much what others think.'

'It must have skipped a generation.'

'I have no…' he snapped his fingers as he searched for the word '…no doubt.' He shook his head, clearly not happy with his choice. 'No guilt…' Still he frowned.

'No qualms.' Emma stared coolly at him. 'The word you're looking for is *qualms*.'

'It was the D'Amilo name that made our current directors rich, it is my acumen that has lined their pockets, and it is *my* brain that keeps it that way. I have no *qualms* about fighting for what is rightfully mine.'

'Modest, too.' Emma's mouth twisted. She was way past even pretending to be polite now. She didn't have time for this. There was no way she was going to agree, and there was no way he was going to lend her the money. She should never have come back!

'I don't believe in false modesty,' Zarios continued. 'I am the best—it is as simple as that.'

He sat down then, and stared at her as if commencing a business meeting.

'I will transfer the funds you require into your account now; in return we will go to my father tonight and tell him of our plans.'

'And what happens when your father realises it was just a charade?' Emma asked scathingly.

'Who said anything about a charade?' Zarios frowned. 'We *will* be engaged.'

'But when it ends…' Emma flailed.

'It might not!' Zarios just laughed at her confusion. 'There is, after all, a high possibility we will get married!'

'Married…' She scooped up her bag. She had never heard anything more bizarre in her life. She loved Jake and would do anything to help him—well, almost anything—but a marriage of convenience with a snake like Zarios was way beyond the call of sisterly duty.

'You're hardly in a position to walk out,' Zarios called to her departing back.

'I'm in every position. You really think I'd marry *you*? After all you've done, the way you are, do you really think I'd want to be married to a man like you?'

'I never said that you *had* to marry me.'

'You just did.' Her fingers were reaching for the door handle. She was in absolutely no mood to decipher one of Zarios's cryptic messages—in no state to have her frayed emotions toyed with even for a little while longer.

'If you would let me finish—you will see you *do* have an exit clause.'

'An exit clause…' She blinked in anger and frustration at his businesslike terms. His utter disregard for the sanctity of marriage had never been more evident.

'Your parents' insurance payout, the funds from their house—all are due for settlement around the same time as the board's decision.' Warily Emma nodded. 'If you pay me back on the day you receive your inheritance you can walk away as soon as the board announces its decision.'

'That's all?' Emma frowned, turning around to look at him. 'I just have to pay you back?'

'That's it.'

'But what about your father?'

'I'll worry about that.'

'But it will devastate him…'

'You have delusions of grandeur, Emma. I don't think *devastate* is the word—I am sure we will all survive. Anyway, we are talking about a hypothetical situation—one I don't believe will transpire. As I said, I have every reason to believe we *will* be married.'

'Zarios, I will pay you back.' She couldn't really believe she was talking as if this was going to happen. 'You know what I'm due to receive, and I always pay my debts…'

'They *are* your debts?'

She swallowed, a dart of nervousness flashing in her eyes. Of course Jake would pay her back—she'd get it in writing this time, Emma decided. She'd get him to sign an agreement that he would pay her back in full on the day their parents' inheritance came through.

'You'll get your money.'

'We'll see.' Zarios smiled. 'Until I do, you will be my fiancée. You will move in to my home so that I can take care of you—or rather deal with the press and the questions…'

'I won't…' Emma flushed. 'I mean, there'll be no…'

'I don't understand what you are saying.' He flashed her an innocent smile.

'Oh, I think you do. I want to make it clear, *very* clear, that we won't be sharing a bed.'

'I think the cleaners might suspect something if my fiancée is sleeping in a separate bed. And, as I said, we will be at my father's this weekend. He found out his son had lost virginity many years ago…'

'Fine!' Emma trilled, her face on fire. 'But we won't be sleeping together.'

'You expect me to sleep on the floor.'

Bastard. The word hissed on her lips, but she swallowed it down. She knew he was goading her, knew he was going to make her say it—well, she would.

'There will be no sex—and I want an assurance from you that there will be no pressure.'

'Pressure?' For the first time that day she heard Zarios laugh. He actually threw his head back and laughed at her statement. But Emma stood her ground.

'You can add *that* to your precious clauses,' Emma spat.

'Why?' He stood up and walked towards her. 'Why waste my lawyer's time getting him to write up a rule that is only going to be broken?'

'It won't be.'

'And as for pressure…' He wasn't laughing now. 'Be careful what you accuse me of, Emma.'

He was in her face now, so close she could smell him even as she backed further towards the door. His dangerous gaze held hers, black fading to indigo, just as it had on the morning he had saved her. Only now it felt as if she were drowning again—drowning in this man who could blind her to his faults. She dragged her eyes downwards, but there was no solace to be had there. His full mouth was moving in on her as he warned her to choose her words more carefully, as he made a mockery of the one rule she had insisted upon.

'I have never, will never, pressure a woman.'

'Good.' Her voice was a croak, but somehow she got the word out. His hand was behind her now, lazily holding the door she leant against. There was not a shred of contact between them, but she felt as if he was inside her.

'Do you feel pressured now?'

His mouth was mere inches from hers, her mind was quailing, but her treacherous body flared in an instant recall of their one dizzy time together.

'You haven't answered the question…' Zarios said slowly. 'Emma, am I pressuring you now?'

'No.'

'Do you want me to kiss you?'

Yes.

She didn't say it, but the word snapped like a twig between them.

She wanted to forget, to escape…for just one moment. To forget this living hell and taste the heaven she had once witnessed. To accept the temporary relief his mouth would surely provide.

To be held instead of holding up.

He kissed her then, his mouth crushing hers. Except she was kissing him back with all her might, pressing her body into his as if she wanted to climb inside him to escape, revelling in the freedom that his touch, his kiss, his *being* somehow brought her. Oh, she was lost, lost, lost, and it was wonderful. She was back in oblivion and it tasted divine. His tongue stroked hers, extricated her from the hell of the past few weeks. *How* she kissed him back—biting on his lip, sucking his flesh, holding his head as he held hers. They were devouring each other with hot, angry kisses that soothed.

The ferocity of his erection pressed into her groin just wasn't enough. The incessant pressure of his mouth, the delicious probing of his tongue and the contentious feel of his hand pushing up her skirt, creeping along her thigh, was bliss. Yet it still wasn't enough! And he knew, *he knew*, because his fingers were hard on the soft flesh of her inner thigh. She parted them, just moved her feet a fraction, and still he kissed her, still his fingers crept higher, till they arrived at her sweet, welcoming moist warmth. As he slid his fingers inside her, his skilled hand dimmed reason. She pulled her head away from his kiss, biting on his shoulder or else she'd scream, knowing that in just a second she would come in his hand.

And then he stopped. His cruel withdrawal momentarily stunning her.

'As I said…' His free hand lifted her chin so he could

look at her, even as still he held her in the palm of his hand. 'I do not waste my time with rules I know will be broken.'

As he removed his hand, hers met his cheek. Tears, hate, shame and loathing—all were there in her aim. Not just for him, but for the betrayal of her own body, that even after all he had done still she could want him.

He didn't even flinch, just walked to his computer, four livid strokes where her fingers had been on his cheek.

Her phone was buzzing in her bag. Her body was twitching and confused at the withdrawal of his affection. Her mind was begging her to get out, warning her that she might as well make a deal with the devil himself rather than enter into this with Zarios.

And yet…

When everything had gone, there was nothing left to lose.

'I have one condition…'

'I thought we just dealt with that.'

'There will be no other women.' Emma swallowed hard. 'As long as this charade continues, as long you are engaged or married to me, there are to be no other women or the deal is off.'

He gave a surly shrug.

'I mean it…' Emma shivered. 'You are not to see anyone else. I won't be humili…' Her voice trailed off. It was a bit late for that.

'Fine,' he clipped. 'I am as good as my word—and here it is. If during our time together I sleep with another woman then you can walk away without owing me a cent. Now…' he turned his face to the screen to conclude the messy business '…can I have your bank details?'

'I hate what you did to me,' Emma said, just to be

sure he knew it. But Zarios was as unmoved as he was unimpressed.

'Your bank details, Emma?'

She hated herself even more for giving them.

CHAPTER SEVEN

'YOU'VE got it?' Jake was pale with relief. 'I can ring them…you can transfer it now…'

'Why don't I just deposit it into your account?'

'For Beth to see?'

'She's going to find out, Jake. Once the inheritance goes through, you're going to have to explain why there isn't any…'

'That's weeks away.' Jake shook his head.

'It's two weeks away, Jake. And you can deny it all you like, but this problem isn't going to go away. Beth *has* to be told.'

'I know that,' Jake shrilled. 'I know that. But I can't tell her now, Em. Not with the way things are. If Beth and I can just get past this… And anyway…' his face crumpled in despair '…I don't trust myself with that sort of money…'

'You're getting help?'

'I'm going to meetings every day… I haven't gambled in weeks.'

Her bank details jumped up on the screen and Emma swallowed, reeling at the balance, her fingers hovering over the keyboard as Jake read out his loan shark's details.

'You *have* to pay me back, Jake.'

'You know I will.'

'No, Jake, I don't.' She turned to face her brother. 'I want it in writing. I want the money you owe me to go directly into my bank account when the settlement goes through.'

'Are you saying you don't trust me?'

'I *don't* trust you, Jake.' After what she'd had to go through today, it wasn't hard to say. 'I don't trust you with money—I'd be an absolute fool to. I need it in writing.'

'Fine!' he snapped, ripping out a piece of paper from her printer and scrawling a note stating the sum that was being borrowed, and that he would pay her back at the time of their settlement. 'Satisfied?'

Emma took the piece of paper and placed it in her bag, hardly able to make out the digits on the keyboard as her eyes swam with tears. She knew the second she hit 'confirm' she was truly indebted to Zarios. For the next two weeks she was a pawn in the elaborate game he was playing—conning poor Rocco.

'Never do this again, Jake. I will *never* help you again.'

'I'll never ask.'

And he meant it. Staring into eyes that were as blue as her own, seeing the wretchedness in his features, the shame, the grief, the embarrassment, she knew that he meant it and reached out her arms to her brother.

'I'm so ashamed…' he sobbed. 'I hate myself more than you hate me.'

'I don't hate you, Jake. I'm just scared for you.'

'I miss them, Em.'

'I know.'

'They'd be so ashamed…'

'Don't think about that.'

'I'll make them proud.' He was a snivelling mess, his grief, his shame, his fear so raw, so real, that surely, *surely* this was his rock bottom? Surely this had to be the last time? 'I'm never gambling again. I'm going to make you proud—make Beth and the twins proud…'

'Make *yourself* proud, Jake.' She gave a tired smile as he glanced at his watch.

'I've got a meeting…'

'Then go.'

'How *did* you get Zarios to agree?'

'It doesn't matter.' Emma gave a thin smile. 'You've got the money.'

'Thank you.'

Jake wasn't the only one with an important meeting to attend. Staring out of her window Emma watched as Zarios's sleek silver car purred up to the kerb. She could almost sense that he knew the money had just been spent.

That she was now his.

That thought was confirmed when, instead of opening his car door, instead of walking down the path to her flat, Zarios gave a short burst on his horn that told her, as if she didn't already know, he was here.

That he had come to claim what he now owned.

'Emma!' Rocco rose from his chair and embraced her. 'It is good of you to come and see me…'

The house was just as it always was whenever Emma went there. Situated in the exclusive Melbourne suburb of Toorak. The door had been opened by Roula, Rocco's elderly housekeeper, and she had walked them through the home which was more like a vast mausoleum to his brief marriage—its walls and surfaces lined with images of their brief union.

Emma was shocked at the frailty of Rocco as he held her. In the few weeks since she'd last seen him he'd aged more than a decade, and Emma knew it wasn't just his illness he was suffering from, but a broken heart—he'd loved her parents, too.

'You should have told me you were bringing Emma over,' Rocco scolded his son.

'What, and spoil the surprise?' Zarios smiled.

'I am too old for surprises.'

'You're sixty,' Zarios pointed out, but it was hopeless. Age really was just a number, and despite his wealth, despite the trappings they afforded, the years really had ravaged his father.

'Emma is staying tonight,' Zarios informed Rocco. 'She needs a break, and there is also something—'

'You should have said—I will tell Roula to make up a room, that we have a guest…'

'There is no need to make up a room for a guest. Emma is family,' Zarios corrected him, and Emma noticed the slight swallow before he continued. 'Or she will be soon.'

A smudge of a frown flickered over Rocco's brow. 'You two?'

'Yes.'

'Are together?' Still Rocco frowned. 'Since when?'

'Since Eric's birthday.'

'But what about Miranda…'

'That is why I ended it with Miranda, Pa…'

'Why didn't you say?' Rocco's voice was bemused. 'Why did you let me think the filth in the papers was true?'

'We wanted to be sure…' Zarios took her hand and Emma realised he was as skilled a liar as he was a lover. 'Pa, we know how big this is, and we had to be sure. With everything that has happened these past few weeks, as terrible as they have been, it has helped us to make up our minds. I have asked Emma to marry me, and happily she has agreed.'

He would lie at his own father's grave, Emma thought, and then realised with a cold drench of horror that in effect she was doing the same: manipulating this wonderful man who, as Rocco's eyes sought hers for clarification, perhaps trusted Emma more than he did his own son.

'Is this true?' Rocco asked. 'You two really are engaged?'

She could feel Zarios's hand tighten around hers, attempting to provoke a response, but all she could manage was the tiniest nod.

'We are going to get a ring tomorrow…' Zarios filled in the long silence. 'We wanted to tell you before the papers got hold of it.'

'And you are happy?' Rocco asked, still more stunned than pleased.

Even when Roula, the housekeeper, was duly summoned, when champagne was poured and toasts given, there was a forced joviality about it all—and not just from Emma.

Rocco, she realised, was clearly choosing to reserve judgement—he was wary with his words, thin with his sentiment—and for the first time Emma glimpsed what Zarios had meant when he had said that his relationship with his father wasn't one she could understand. On the night his only son had announced his engagement, after a cursory glass of champagne and some rather strained small talk and stilted interaction between father and son, Rocco reminded Zarios of the time in Europe, and that he had an important call that needed to be made.

'I shouldn't be long.' Zarios glanced at his watch, and then to Emma, and for the first time she saw just a flicker of nervousness in his eyes. No doubt he was worried at leaving her alone with his father.

'Avetti is an important client…' Rocco waved him away. 'You will take as long as is necessary.'

Pensively, Rocco smiled over at Emma, once they were alone. 'You must have mixed feelings at a time like this?'

'I do.' Emma nodded, able to look him in the eye now, because for that second in time she was telling the truth.

'Come!' He stood up and gestured to a large dresser, where Emma joined him. 'I found this photo of your father and I just the other week, when I was going through some papers. You will not have seen it—I didn't even know I had it.'

She smiled at the image of two grubby little boys sitting on a wall, their knees grazed and dirty. It hurt almost too much to look at the image of her father, so she focused instead on Rocco. As dark as Zarios, but with a cheeky grin, there was a lightness about him Emma could never imagine in his son.

She was right—there in the another photo was Zarios, at eight or nine years old, refusing to smile for his school photo, looking as serious and as accusing as he did now.

'He hated boarding school.' Rocco interrupted her thoughts. 'I hated sending him. I thought I was doing the right thing by him at the time—it is a choice I regret.'

Hearing the wistful note in Rocco's voice, seeing his kind, tired eyes, reminded her so much of her dad it made her brave enough for an observation. 'You don't seem pleased, Rocco, about the engagement?'

'I am torn,' Rocco admitted. 'I love my son, but…' He frowned, more to himself than to Emma. 'Your parents meant the world to me. In some ways with them gone I feel more responsible towards you—almost as if you were a daughter. If I could forget for a moment that Zarios was my son, as much as I love him, I have to be honest— I am not sure he is what I would wish for my daughter…'

Which was hardly a glowing reference from a father, but it was said with more concern than malice. His eyes filled with tears as they came to rest on another photo. Emma followed his gaze, her throat tightening, because there, in contrast to the austere photo of his youth, was a very different Zarios.

A smiling, happy little boy, three, maybe four years old, running along the beach carrying a plastic windmill.

And there he was again, grinning and laughing, wrapped in his mother's arms, with a smiling Rocco looking proudly on.

A different Zarios and a different Rocco, too.

'You would never have met Bella.' Rocco picked up the photo and gazed at it fondly, then handed it to Emma. 'Our marriage broke up before you were even born.'

'She's beautiful.'

'She was…' Rocco smiled. 'She was also way too young to be married. She was just sixteen. Things were different in those days. The marriage was arranged by my grandparents—Bella was from my village back home. She came to Australia speaking no English.'

'As you did.'

'I was younger. I picked up the language more easily—and I had friends like your father to help me. Bella was just lost. I tried to make things easier on her, but she never settled. Now, when I look back, I think she must have been depressed after Zarios was born. But in those days we didn't really understand or talk about such things. I tried to make it work. We went back to Italy, but still she was unhappy.'

'So Zarios went to boarding school…?'

'And I came back here.' He nodded at the question in her voice. 'Here was the only place I could make the money to pay the fees and support my family, too…the lucky country!' He shook his head sadly. 'It didn't feel like it. I went back to Italy as often as I could, opened a business there, but here was where the money was being made. Of course I hoped his mother might be around more for him…'

It was unfathomable to Emma. She thought of her own happy childhood, of her parents who, even with their faults, would have moved heaven and earth for her, and wondered, just as her parents had over the years, how Bella could have excluded herself so totally from her son's life.

'More than anything I want Zarios to be happy. Always the hurt is there—always with Zarios anger. I want my son to find the love that has been missing for most of his life. You *do* love my son, Emma?'

Rocco's question was direct, his eyes so searching that she shouldn't be able to answer it. But, looking down to the photo she held in her hands, Emma knew she wanted to see Zarios happy, too. Wanted back what they had found that morning. Wanted the man she knew was there beneath the pomp and scorn. Wanted the merry dark eyes that danced in this photograph, that she was sure she had glimpsed that wonderful morning, to dance for her again.

There was no doubt she was indebted to him, and not just financially—he had saved her life when she'd nearly drowned, had held her hand when she'd identified her parents, had sat and offered quiet support that first long, lonely night.

Tears coursed down her cheeks, but not for the reason Rocco thought. Emma realised as she nodded, as she told Rocco what he wanted to hear, that she was actually speaking the truth.

She loved him.

She hated him, but somehow had loved him over the years—had loved him that one wonderful morning together—and despite all that had been said, all that was, all that could never be, still somehow she loved him.

'Then you will both be okay—love is what will see you through,' Rocco said wisely. 'Love is what was missing in my marriage. Not,' he added sadly, 'on my side. For my son to have asked for your hand in marriage, he must love you, too.'

Oh, she wished that this were true, that Zarios *did* love her, did want to rescue her from the hell of these past weeks.

Wished that it were that simple.

'You're quiet,' Zarios noted when finally they were alone and could let down the charade as the bedroom door closed behind them.

'I'm tired.' Emma sat at the dressing table and wearily attempted to remove her make-up while Zarios unashamedly undressed behind her. Tired was an understatement. She had been running on adrenaline since her meeting with Zarios, had been sitting on tenterhooks all evening as her head throbbed with a low-grade headache, and her mind was too tired to even attempt to make sense of what she had agreed to. 'Actually, I've got a headache.'

'Isn't it a bit early in our relationship to be making such excuses?' It was said so tongue in cheek and with such irony that as she caught his glance in the mirror Emma couldn't help but smile. But it faded. 'What *will* your dad say when he finds out?'

'What can he say?' Zarios shrugged.

Instead of the naked figure she had been sure she'd be sleeping with, he had pulled on a pair of black pyjama bottoms—only they did nothing to detract from his beauty. Even in the dimmed bedroom light she could see his reflection in the mirror, his body muscled and gleaming, the pants making him look like some martial arts expert, and just as toned and dangerous. Leaving on her panties, she pulled on a T-shirt and climbed into bed beside him. Turning off the light and rolling on her side, she braced herself for his onslaught—it never came. His breathing settled, and his body just relaxed beside hers as Emma lay twitching and restless, positive that the second she lowered her guard, allowed the heavy drape of sleep that was closing in to wrap around her, then Zarios would surely pounce.

Only he didn't.

The usual shot of adrenaline that had been her bedmate since her parents' death catapulted her awake at 4:00 a.m., but instead of sitting bolt upright and grappling for the light switch, having to relieve the nightmare all over again as she gulped down a drink of water, an arm heavy with sleep wrapped around her, sliding her across the bed in one easy movement. At first Emma was so stunned she didn't resist, just lay in his arms, her heart pounding. She was infinitely grateful for the contact, felt the fear seeping out of her as his solid presence soothed.

'Go back to sleep, Emma.' His low voice growled a welcome order as an idle hand stroked her hair, and she wished she could obey—wished she could close her eyes and desist. Only an unchecked niggle was scratching, reminding her of his distaste when she'd walked into his office—of his first assumption as to the reason she was there.

Wandering back into the forest, tentatively she searched for that arrow he had aimed.

She had *definitely* had her period on the day of the funeral.

Her body was spooned into his—Zarios's heavy arm across her waist, his hand loosely dusting her stomach, like any normal couple in bed. She struggled for a second against his unwitting affection, but deep in slumber, too comfortable to move, Zarios gripped her tighter. Emma stumbled deeper into the wilderness, locating the arrow and staring at a segment of her shattered heart. Tentatively she probed it.

She'd had her period that day, but it was six... She screwed her eyes tightly closed as she did the maths. No, it was eight weeks now since she'd had another.

'*Dorme...*' Zarios mumbled, pulling her closer towards him. 'Sleep now.'

It was easier to ignore it, easier to cover the remains with leaves rather than probe it with a stick, to just lie in his arms and do as he told her.

Even the lazy tumescence of his manhood that stirred as he dreamed didn't startle Emma. Instead the naturalness of it soothed.

Feeling him asleep but *alive* beside her, it was easy, too easy, to forget what had brought them to this point.

Maybe she was more like Jake than she realised. Because it was easier to forget about her problems than try to solve them—easier to just close her eyes and drift back to sleep, with Zarios there beside her...

CHAPTER EIGHT

DESPITE her mother's theories, even in her art student days wild parties hadn't been a regular feature on Emma's agenda.

But waking in Zarios's arms Emma got a taste of how it must feel to wake after a walk on the wild side. Every sin she had ever committed, and surely a few more to come, seemed to be laughing from the sidelines as she awoke in a strange bed, in the arms of the man she'd sworn away from.

'What time is it?' Zarios grumbled as she stirred awake beside him.

'Are we still engaged?' Emma winced, trying to do up the pieces of the jigsaw without the aid of a picture.

'We are.' His hot breath on the back of her neck somehow told her he was smiling. 'And, yes, you *do* owe me an obscene amount of money.'

As she rolled over to face him she hoped, actually prayed, for a whiff of bad breath, for something horrible and nasty to greet her—but her prayers went unanswered. It was Zarios! Just as gorgeous as yesterday, except he seemed to have grown a beard overnight, morning shadow dense on his strong jaw. The other change in him was that for once he was smiling—this was a far more relaxed Zarios than the one she was used to seeing.

And though sensibly she knew she should recoil, there was this lovely mesh of legs… Such a mesh that Emma didn't know where hers were, though she had a vague idea where his were, because she could feel the bit in the middle as it sort of rose to her groin to say good morning.

'Morning.' His eyes smiled their greeting just inches from hers. And she'd forgotten to notice his mouth—such a lovely soft, full lipped mouth—that was somehow on the same pillow…

'Morning.'

'You talk in your sleep,' Zarios said.

'You snore!' Emma countered.

'I don't.'

He didn't.

'Why are beds so much more comfortable in the morning?' Emma asked, after a few lovely moments of just lying there. 'I mean, you spend half the night trying to get comfortable, but in the morning, when it's time to get up…'

'Don't get up, then,' Zarios said, nudging the duvet up around them with his shoulder and then promptly closing his eyes.

There was a strange fuzzy logic going on in her head—she could feel his tumescent manhood between them, felt so warm and safe lying with him. It would be so easy to accept the lazy kiss she knew was coming, so easy not to deny the fierce attraction that was undoubtedly between them—but at what cost?

The pain of losing him to Miranda had her rolling on her back. Emma stared at the ceiling, hearing the grumble of his sleepy protest. How much easier it would be for him, how much more *pleasant* it would make it for him, to have her on tap these two weeks. And how appalling for her it would be when it ended—to face once more the obstacle course of getting over him!

It was with that in mind that she hauled herself out of bed and headed for the shower.

'How did you sleep?' Rocco asked as Roula poured the coffee.

'Very well!' Emma answered politely, smiling into her cup at Zarios's surly expression. He was clearly rattled that for once his impressive charm hadn't worked.

'So what are your plans today? You are going to get a ring? And then what, Emma? Will you be working, or…?'

'Emma's taking a break from work for a little while…' Zarios answered for her. 'Since her parents' death her painting hasn't been going well. She needs a break.'

'Good!' Rocco nodded. 'What about you, Zarios? You are in Melbourne this week, Singapore the next… You could do some shopping…' He smiled fondly at Emma, but again Zarios had it all worked out.

'We have the ball in Sydney. Emma will be preparing for that.'

'And then the board meets…' Rocco's eyes narrowed just a fraction as he looked over to his son, and for that fleeting moment Emma was sure he had worked their scam out. 'I spoke to your mother last night, Zarios.'

'You called her?' His words were like pistol shots, the ambient mood at the table suddenly plunging. 'Why?'

'Our son is getting engaged—it is right that she is told.'

'She lost her right to be informed thirty years ago.'

Incensed, he stood up. 'Why would you do that? Why would you even *think* to call her?'

'Actually, I didn't call her,' Rocco responded calmly. 'Your mother called me. You know she has been calling for the last few months…'

'Since she found out you were sick!' Zarios sneered. 'Can't you see what she is doing?'

'Is it impossible for you to believe she might regret what happened?'

'Yes,' came Zarios's curt reply.

'She wants to ring you tonight—to congratulate you herself.'

'Tell her not to bother.'

You need to forgive your mother, Zarios.'

'It's rather hard without even an apology from her,' Zarios said, standing up. 'Come,' he called over to Emma as he strode out of the room, 'we have to get going…'

'I thought you were staying the weekend?' Rocco said.

'I'm not staying to watch you being made a fool of—and I have *nothing* to say to your ex-wife!'

Rocco gave Emma a tight smile at the fading sound of Zarios climbing the stairs.

'It must be hard for him.'

'She has never had more children, and she has never settled down. She hates herself for what she did, but she was ill…. *Am* I a fool, Emma?' Sad, tired eyes searched Emma's for an answer she simply couldn't give. 'Am I a fool to believe she might actually be talking to me now because she cares?'

'I've never met her…' Emma said helplessly. 'Only you can answer that, Rocco.'

'You'd better go.' Rocco kissed her on the cheek, as

he always did, then cuddled her for a moment. 'He does need to forgive her, Emma. And not just for my sake—it is not good for him to carry so much hate in his heart. Talk to him…'

Which was an impossible task.

Any closeness that had been captured in the night had long since faded. Zario was driving back into the city as if the devil himself were chasing them, in absolutely no mood for a pep talk. Though she did try!

'He was right to tell her. I mean, if your father does believe we're really engaged, then of course he was right to tell her!'

'I don't give a damn what he told her,' Zarios cursed loudly, his hand lifting off the steering wheel as if he were swatting a fly. 'It is that he is even talking with the *puttana*…' He stared over at her appalled expression. 'You think I should not talk of my mother like that?'

'Yes! And I also think you're being a bit hard on your father.'

'You do, do you?'

They were sitting at traffic lights, Zarios beating a restless tune on the steering wheel, only talking again when the lights turned green and they were moving again.

'My father did what he had to do. There was no work in his village, and he had no family in Australia to help with me. I accept why he left me in Italy. But that woman he calls my mother…' Zarios shook his head. 'She has never been a mother, and it's too late to start now—way too late to start playing happy families just because my father is now sick. If he cannot see she is using him, then I am only too happy to point it out!'

'He deserves to be happy…'

'Emma!' Zarios snapped. 'If you were my *real* fiancée perhaps your opinion would be warranted. Unwelcome,' he added, 'but possibly warranted. But, given that you're not…'

They were pulling up outside The Casino, a valet parker making his way over, and Emma felt herself shrink into the seat.

'Why are we here?'

'To find you a ring,' Zarios answered, watching her closely as he spoke. 'To sort out your clothes and get your hair styled—we can do all that here. Is there a problem?'

Her heart was fluttering in her chest, her eyes wide as she watched the flurry of activity in the foyer. The Casino was a jewel in Melbourne's crown, hugging the Yarra River, and filled with lavish restaurants, designer boutiques and exclusive jewellers. And it was positively the last place Emma wanted to be. On many occasion she'd spent endless hours searching the gaming rooms there for Jake. Despite his alleged clean slate, still deep inside Emma couldn't relax—couldn't help wondering if Jake was here now, creating more debts.

'Do you have a problem being here, Emma?' There was an edge to Zarios's voice that she didn't understand.

'Of course not…' Emma tried to keep her voice light as her car door was opened, but knew she'd failed.

Zarios certainly made heads turn.

As they walked through the humming foyer, Emma could feel the glare of the spotlight his mere presence created. His aura caused people to frown as they tried to place him, or just to take a long, lingering look at a truly impressive specimen of man. Not that Zarios seemed to notice the stir he created. He merely dispatched Emma to a very exclusive beauty salon and had the nerve to tell the beautician what he was hoping she could achieve.

'Can I leave you here, then?'

Emma shot him a withering look. 'Tell me a time to meet you and I'll be there.'

'We will meet here,' Zarios said. 'And if you do finish early, please try and restrain yourself.'

She had no idea what he was talking about—just slipped into a gown while he went off and did whatever it was that people like Zarios did. Emma sat while her straight blonde hair was shot through with layers and caramel foils added. Then, when her hair was deemed suitable, her complexion that had been so ravaged these past weeks, from sleepless nights and too much crying, was given the attention it craved, along with the mammoth task of getting rid of the bags under her eyes.

Gone!

Staring in the mirror, waiting for Zarios, Emma could only marvel. Weeks of pain had been wiped away. Her hair was glossy and shiny, with chunky, angular layers giving it an up-to-date edge. The perfect hair and new make-up gave her a sophisticated air that belied the terrified, grieving child inside.

Zarios didn't comment when he came to collect her—his mood clearly hadn't improved, and neither had Emma's. She felt like a puppy being picked up from the kennel.

Humiliatingly, he paid the bill and then led her downstairs to a very exclusive jeweller, which looked, to Emma's untrained eyes, to be closed.

Zarios pushed on the intercom and growled out his name. It was clearly the abracadabra word, because the thick black glass doors parted.

'Mr D'Amilo…' A suited gentleman greeted them politely, ushering them to waiting chairs. An assistant entered with two glasses of champagne and an arrangement of chocolates, before the serious business of choosing a ring began. Emma hesitantly tried a couple on with the encouragement of the jeweller, as Zarios sat drumming his fingers on his thigh as he did when he was bored.

'They're all beautiful…' Emma gulped. 'What do you think?' Her eyes turned to his, silently pleading with him for some help, but his uninterest was embarrassingly apparent, causing Emma to flush in front of the jeweller.

'Does that one fit?' Zarios pointed to the one she was wearing.

'Don't worry about size—' the jeweller began, but Zarios's mind was already made up.

'I think my fiancée has chosen.'

He didn't even have to hand over his credit card! Zarios, Emma was fast realising, lived in the world of the seriously rich, where no money or signature was either exchanged or required. No doubt an invoice would be sent *somewhere* and dealt with by *somebody*.

As they stepped out Emma could feel tears stinging her eyes. Rather than letting them fall, she sniffed loudly.

'What's wrong?' Zarios said irritably.

'Could you have made it any more obvious in there?' Emma sniffed again, then checked herself.

'Made what obvious?'

'That we're not a couple—that we don't... It doesn't matter.'

'Clearly it does,' Zarios observed, then stopped walking, turning to face her. But they were blocking an aisle, and Zarios moved her out of the current to the entrance of a shop. 'How do you *want* me to be?'

'I'm just saying that in public...'

'Am I not affectionate enough for you?' There was a dangerous glint to his eyes.

'It's not that.' His face was so close she could barely breathe, her thought processes dizzied by his proximity.

'Would you rather I was more demonstrative?'

'No!' Emma shrilled. 'But if we are going to pretend, then at least you could look as if you care...'

'You confuse me, Emma.' His face was coming nearer so she backed away, leaning against the shop window. She was confused herself as to what it was she was saying, what it was that she wanted, but Zarios was rapidly enlightening her! 'You tell me to leave you alone, you dress like a gypsy for bed—and you certainly didn't want my attentions this morning—but now, suddenly, when I am observing your wishes, you accuse me of not being demonstrative enough.'

'We're supposed to be engaged...' Emma swallowed. 'We're supposed to look as if we're in love. Yet you snapped your fingers at me in the hairdressers, you couldn't have been less interested in the choice of ring, and you didn't even hold my hand!' Oh, what was the point? Shaking her head, she went to stalk off—but *now* he caught her hand and held it.

'Is that better?'

'No!' She stared down at their entwined fingers, at the obnoxiously large ring that had been placed there in the name of business only, unable to hold the tears back. 'I'm ashamed enough by what we're doing, even though I have my reasons for doing it…' There was a stoicism about her, despite the tears. 'But I'm not *that* good an actress, Zarios. If my real fiancé ever treated me or spoke to me in that way, I'd walk!'

'Fair enough!' For once it wasn't a flip comment. 'You're right—it does not look good—and for what it's worth, if you were *my* real fiancée, I'd expect you to walk… Hey…' he added as her tears fell further. 'My fiancée crying in the street is not a good look either.' But there was almost a smudge of kindness hidden in his pompous voice.

'They're tears of joy!' The irony of her words actually eked a smile from his haughty face. 'Just don't treat me like a lapdog…' Emma sniffed '…don't embarrass me further than I already am.'

He loosened his grip from her hand and with the pads of his thumbs wiped away the tears on her cheeks so tenderly it almost felt as if he meant it.

'Is that better?'

'Yes.'

'You're sure?' Zarios checked.

'Quite sure.'

'And if I did embarrass you in there…' his mouth lowered to hers, kissing her clamped unmoving mouth slowly and very, very surely as she stood there rigid '…then I was wrong.' He moved his face away just a fraction. 'I will remember to behave better in public next time.'

He was still just as appalling in private, though.

He ignored her request to stop at her flat and grab some things. 'You don't need them—you have nice things now!' Zarios said, pinging open the car boot once they had slid into the forecourt of a luxury five-star hotel.

'Where *are* we?'

'Home.'

She felt like a beggar girl as boxes and bags were hauled out of the boot by the bellboys, and King Cophetua led her by the hand briskly though the lobby, where they were whizzed to the Presidential Suite.

'You *live* here?'

'Sometimes,' Zarios said, dropping his jacket as he did so, and kicking off his shoes as he walked. He stretched out on the settee in the lounge, flicking a remote control. Instead of the television coming on, the drapes lifted to reveal the most stunning view out over the city and beyond to the bay. 'I divide my time between many cities. It makes sense to stay in hotels rather than maintaining several homes.'

Of all the surprises Zarios had thrown at her this was the one, however unwitting, that shocked her the most. Oh, it was luxurious—Emma had never stayed at such an exclusive hotel before, let alone in the Presidential Suite. At every turn it screamed luxury, and as she wandered through, Emma tried to take the details in: the deep sofa, the six-seater oak dining table with a lavish Australian native flower arrangement. The master bedroom was vast, opening into a sparkling marble bathroom, with racks lined with fluffy white towels, two robes hanging on the door just begging for someone to step into them—even soft white slippers patiently waited outside the luxurious two-person shower. Back she wandered, frowning as she realised there was even a small butler's kitchen, and the gnawing disquiet she felt multiplied as Zarios flicked through the room-service menu.

Staring out of the window, she saw Port Phillip Bay stretched like a horseshoe, and her eyes scanned the familiar landmarks that lined it: Brighton Pier, then along to Mentone, and ever on till they came to rest, as they always did, on the gorgeous tip at the end that seemed to be reaching out to embrace Queenscliff. The jagged edge that contained within it her family home.

This wasn't, as first she had thought, Zarios's home within a hotel.

This—despite its luxurious furnishings, despite the impressive artwork that lined the walls—*was* just a hotel room. A room that when Zarios left would be painstakingly prepared for the next well-heeled guest to stay.

Emma's eyes were so thick with tears that she could hardly make out her home now—but even if it was being sold in two weeks, even if her parents had gone way too soon, even if she was indebted to Zarios, still she was richer than he had ever been.

Even if she'd mourn them for ever, at least she'd had a family, and at least she'd had a home.

Which were two luxuries that Zarios had never been afforded.

CHAPTER NINE

'It's just a dream, Emma.'

By unspoken consent it was the only time he held her. When nightmares crept in, so, too, did his hand, bringing her back to reality and then holding her for the rest of the scary night. It had never been discussed, and for that Emma was grateful. She was just surprised each and every night by just how *nice* he could be when he wanted—by the remarkable tenderness he offered at these times, and the infinite patience he was capable of.

But only at night.

Their first week together had passed in a blur of endless social functions as Melbourne's elite toasted the happy couple. Her days, though, had been long and lonely, while Zarios attacked his formidable workload, leaving Emma to rattle around the Presidential Suite like a marble in a tin.

Stretching in bed now, Emma glanced at the clock, her head pounding after another restless night.

'Morning!'

Emma jumped as she padded through and saw him at the table, dressed and ready for his day, lazily drinking coffee and flicking through his usual mountain of post.

'Sorry.' He grinned at her startled expression. 'Were you hoping I'd already gone?'

'Not at all.' Emma gave him a sweet smile, buttering some toast even though she didn't feel like it, shaking her head as Zarios picked up the coffee pot.

'I'll have tea.'

'Since when?' Zarios frowned. 'You *always* have coffee.'

'We've only been engaged for a week,' Emma pointed out.

'Full of surprises.' Zarios grinned again, but there was a glint to it which she chose to ignore. 'So, what are you doing today?'

'I'm not sure.'

'The tickets have arrived for next Saturday's ball—which reminds me.' Zarios glanced up. 'You need to get something to wear.'

'I have a wardrobe full of new things to wear,' Emma retorted, but Zarios wasn't listening. He just took a rather loud slurp of his coffee, which set Emma's teeth on edge.

'Sorry, darling!' Zarios said, which told her he wasn't. 'That's the awful sort of habit that should only slip in once you're safely married.'

'Which we'll never be!' Emma said, pouring her tea and adding a heaped spoon of sugar. She watched as Zarios ripped up an engagement congratulations card, which she could only assume was from his mother, and carried on with the rest of his mail.

'Oh, I don't know…' He slurped his coffee again, and Emma realised that he was toying with her. '*When* are you paying me back again?'

'Next Monday,' Emma answered coolly—refusing to

rise to whatever bait he was dangling, picking up a newspaper and reading the headlines.

'Good!' Zarios said, watching as she turned the pages, still too new to the game to be bored with the novelty of seeing her name in print. 'What are they saying about us today?' he asked.

'The usual…' Emma rolled her eyes. 'I'm your rebound from Miranda, a decoy for the board…' She scanned the words, more interested really in the picture. But it was the same one again! Zarios, Emma had fast realised, was always two steps ahead—the unexpected tenderness he had displayed outside the jewellers had been captured on film, and though he had denied it when Emma had confronted him, she was quite sure he had manufactured the whole thing just so that he could be photographed wiping away her tears of happiness and, as the paper had reported, sealing the deal with a kiss.

'This is a better picture of you…' Still reading his mail, almost distracted, he handed her another tabloid, neatly folded at an open page. Emma felt her insides turn to liquid. 'I think you're going into The Casino gaming rooms—I thought it must have been before last week, but your hair's already done. There's a small piece about you…' He wasn't *pretending* to be distracted now. He was staring over at her, his face loaded with contempt. 'It mentions that you looked as if you were crying when you came out…'

Zarios wasn't just two steps ahead, Emma realised, he was a whole street in front. This, Emma knew as she scanned the offensive article, was the *real* reason he was joining her for breakfast. She'd gone to The Casino looking for Jake. After numerous failed attempts to get through to him panic had gripped her, and Emma had headed to the one place she knew she might find him.

'I know how this must look…what you must think.' Emma ran a worried hand through her hair. 'But I don't have a problem—'

'Well, I do,' he interrupted darkly. 'I deal in people's money, in their investments, their savings… My fiancée staggering out of the gaming rooms isn't quite the image I'm hoping to portray.' She squirmed at his implication. 'I don't want your excuses, and I don't want your reasons—just know that I will not be shamed. Zarios D'Amilo's fiancée does *not* have a gambling problem— there will be an apology in the newspaper tomorrow. Don't make me call in any more favours again. Do you think you can stay away for one more week?'

When all she managed was a rigid nod, he said, 'Good. Don't think as my wife you will have access to limitless funds to feed your filthy habit.' Picking up his briefcase he turned to go, but thought better of it. 'I'm assuming that *will* be the case? I mean,' he added nastily, 'people don't usually come out of a casino crying when they've won!'

'You're so quick to think the worst…' She didn't have to justify herself to him—didn't have to beg his understanding or forgiveness for a crime she hadn't even committed. 'You're so sure that everyone's out for your precious dollar!'

'Remind us both again—exactly *why* are you here, Emma? Even before we got into this you told me yourself that was the only thing you wanted from me!'

'After you had gone back to *her*!' Tears stung her eyes as she veered towards the truth. 'You slept with me and then went back to *her*, Zarios. What did you *want* me to say? Congratulations? I hope the two of you will be happy—or the three of you, or whatever made you deem it necessary to just walk away?'

'Leave it, Emma…' Zarios warned, but she wasn't listening.

'You hurt me, Zarios, and I said those things to hurt *you*.'

'That morning…' His usually swarthy face was pale, his jaw so quilted with tension she could see the effort it took for him to form words. 'It was never my intention to go back to her. Miranda told me… I found out that she was…' He shook his head hopelessly. 'Leave it, Emma,' he said again.

Oh, but she wouldn't.

'She *was* pregnant?'

'No.'

'Did she have an abortion?' Emma flailed in the dark for an answer. 'Or lose the baby?'

'I've told you!' Zarios roared. 'There was no baby.'

'So it's true, then?' Over and over she'd tried to fathom an excuse for him—told herself that the papers had got it wrong, that the man she happened to love really wasn't that much of a bastard.

Except he was.

'I have every right to say those hateful things.' Through pale strained lips she told him her truth. 'I have every right to hate you—because you threw away what we had for no good reason. And Miranda has every right to hate you, too.'

'Leave her out of it.'

'Just as you did,' Emma spat, 'when she couldn't

provide you with children. Well, guess what, Zarios? You don't deserve them!'

Always Zarios had the last word—always there was a retort or a scathing reply—but not this time. His face was as white as chalk apart from his black angry eyes. He didn't even pick up his briefcase. He just walked towards the door. And if it hadn't been 8:00 a.m.—if she hadn't seen that he had been perfectly lucid just moments earlier—from his stagger Emma would have sworn he had been drinking.

'Zarios!' She called out to him but it was too late. The door had closed behind him without so much as a slam.

Emma was shaking—not just at the venom of her words, but at the effect they had had. She could feel nausea rising, and barely made it to the bathroom in time. Crouching, hugging the bowl, she was more sick than she had ever been in her life. The anger that had been aimed at him was now aimed somehow at herself, at her fury for not being able to accept that he wasn't the man she wanted him to be, was sure he could be.

After rinsing her mouth, Emma made her way back to the lounge, reading again the article that had led them to this row. Heading for the bin, she picked up the card he had tossed away.

The English wasn't great, but Emma was touched at the effort the woman had made.

Emma and Zarios,
It was with happiness I received the good news of your engagement.
Emma, I hope to meet you soon, to share in your joy.
Mamma xxx

What joy?

Emma stared at her luxurious surrounds and realised then that they counted for nothing—the trappings of wealth had done nothing to fade his scars.

Did Bella have any idea what she'd done?

'Well, that was a lot easier.' Blushing and uncomfortable, she attempted a smile as she closed his office door behind her. 'Your assistant didn't even ask me to take a seat.'

'What are you doing here, Emma?' His face was grey now rather than white.

'You forgot your briefcase!' she said brightly, dangling it on her finger. It was a pathetic excuse and they both knew it. 'Damage control, too…' she attempted. 'I thought it might look better if I show my face.'

'My staff knows better than to believe what they read in the newspaper—and, as I said, there will be a retraction and an apology printed tomorrow.'

'Do they work?' Emma sniffed. 'Because if they do, I'd like to try…'

'Let's just leave it.'

'I'm sorry for what I said this morning—about you not deserving children.'

'Can we forget about that, please?'

'Can we?'

'I just did.' He flashed a very on-off smile and Emma would have given anything to go back, anything to have him tease her or goad her—anything rather than this great aching distance that gaped between them.

'I thought we could go for lunch—'

'I have meetings.' Zarios didn't even let her finish. 'Why don't you go shopping…?'

'I don't want to go shopping.' If she sounded petulant, it was from the embarrassment of having him politely refuse the olive branch she was offering.

'You need an outfit for the ball next Saturday. Our company is the major sponsor, and we will both be in the spotlight—it is an important event!'

'So what's the charity?'

'*Scusi?*'

He often did this, Emma had started to realise. If he was playing for time, his excellent English would curiously slip.

'*Che cosa è la carità?*' Emma said sweetly, in her phrasebook Italian, and Zarios raised an eyebrow. She then asked again. 'What's the ball in aid of?'

'A children's charity…' Zarios answered evasively, but there was just a hint of a smile on the edge of his lips as she played him at his own game. 'I assume. So, when did you start to learn Italian?'

'This morning,' Emma admitted. 'I knew you had no idea what the ball was in aid of.'

'Well, I will graciously concede the point.' He picked up his pen, wordlessly dismissing her, but Emma couldn't let it go.

'I was thinking…' she attempted. 'Tonight, when you get home, maybe instead of going out we could stay in…' She was blushing to her roots, as nervous as a teenager attempting her first flirt. 'We could order something nice from room service…'

'Sounds nice…' she could hear the *but* coming even before he actually uttered it '…but I have to work late.'

'Zarios, I'm trying to say sorry here—'

'Emma, please…' He stood up to conclude their meeting, just as he had done the first time she was there. 'I have to get on.'

The only difference was that this time, when she walked through the foyer, the receptionist didn't call her back.

CHAPTER TEN

HE WAS driving way too fast.

For such a dangerous bend of road, Zarios should be crawling along, but instead he took each curve at breakneck speed, taking his hands off the wheel to fiddle with the radio station. Emma shrank back into the passenger seat, trying to tell herself that he did this every day, that he knew every last turn on the cliff road. She knew that every sharp breath she took just incensed him further, only she couldn't stop herself.

'You drive, then.' Zarios slammed on the brakes so violently that the car screeched to a halt. 'If you think you can do so much better…' He held his hands up in a supremely Latin gesture then climbed out of the car, slamming the door behind him, leaving Emma to take the wheel.

She could do this.

Glancing in the rearview mirror, checking the twins were safely strapped in, Emma gave Harriet and Conner a reassuring smile. 'We'll be there soon.' They didn't answer, just blinked back at her, their eyes huge and trusting.

She could do this, Emma told herself again, then

gently pressed her foot on the accelerator—only Zarios's car was way more powerful than her own, and she might just as well have stood on the pedal, because the car was lurching forward, shooting like a bullet from a gun, and there was nothing she could do. Her foot was jammed on the pedal as they shot over the edge and the salty ocean seemed to rise to claim them. The twins were screaming in terror and there was the sound of a baby crying, too. Emma attempted the same, only her voice was frozen within her, the building scream unable to get out...

'Emma.'

As she sat bolt-upright, dragging in air, she felt his arms wrap around her, his deep voice reassuring her, telling her again, as he had these past nights over and over, that she was safe.

'You're dreaming.' He pulled her back beside him, wrapped himself around her and stroked her arm. 'It's just a dream; you're safe, go back to sleep.'

Except she couldn't.

She hadn't seen him since their strained meeting in his office, hadn't even been aware of him climbing in bed beside her, but she was infinitely grateful that he *was* there. Her body trembled in the darkness as she wished that he would touch her, make love to her, take her away from her desperate thoughts for just a little while. But he'd been as good as his word and hadn't pressured her.

Even if sometimes she wished he would.

'You should see a doctor.' It was the first time they'd discussed her nightmares—the first time he'd done anything other than hold her.

'I don't want to take tablets.'

'Maybe just for a week or two,' Zarios pushed. 'You're pale, you're exhausted—please, just go to the doctor and tell him you're not sleeping.'

'I'll think about it.'

Her heart was slowing down now, her breathing settling, and he lay spooned behind her, held her till he was sure that she was asleep, his fingers coiling and then releasing a strand of her hair. He was resisting the urge to bury his head in it, or to wake her and demand that she stop wasting her life.

It was none of his business, Zarios reminded himself.

Whatever mess she was in—well, it was *hers*. In a little less than a week they would both walk away and never have to see each other again.

It killed him to even think about it.

He held her fragile frame against his, wanted to wrap himself like a shield around her and discount everything he had learnt today.

What had that counsellor on the helpline he had rung said?

That addicts were cunning and manipulative... Zarios's eyes were shuttered for a moment. He found it so easy to discount the brutal summing-up, when he was holding her in his arms.

He had been told that she first had to admit to the problem before Zarios could do anything to help.

'Emma?' She stirred into semi-wakefulness as he rolled onto his side and stared down at her. 'Nothing's ever too big that you can't tell me.'

He smiled as her groggy eyes tried to focus on his.

'If there's something worrying you it's better to face it.'

'I know,' she mumbled.

'And,' Zarios ventured on, 'if I can do anything to help, I will.'

'Even after this morning?' Her sleepy voice begged.

'Especially after this morning. Emma.' He was playing with her hair again, but this time it was her fringe, pushing it out of her eyes, feeling the damp stream of tears on her cheeks. He'd have given anything to lower his head and kiss her—would at that moment have given anything for her…

Which was the reason he didn't.

Pressure from any quarter, according to the counsellor, was the very last thing she needed.

CHAPTER ELEVEN

'No, THERE's no chance that I'm pregnant.'

Her GP glanced down at her rather obvious engagement ring, then flicked through Emma's notes. 'I see you're not on the pill.'

'There hasn't—I mean, we haven't—' Emma flushed purple. 'Not since Mum and Dad's accident.'

'Which was about eight weeks ago?' Dr Ross checked.

'Nine weeks now.' Emma gulped. 'I had my period on the day of the funeral.'

'And have you had a period since then?'

'No,' Emma admitted. 'But stress can affect that, and I'm not very regular at the best of times…'

'And you're vomiting?'

'Once or twice,' Emma lied, just a little bit. She could feel her stomach churning now, just from the smell of the coffee on his desk. 'But that's not what I'm here for—it's more about the nightmares—'

'Let's just get a sample…' her GP broke off her ream of excuses with a rather more practical suggestion '…and then we'll talk. I don't want to prescribe anything till we've covered all the bases.'

He was certainly thorough, checking her blood pressure and temperature, listening to her chest, feeling her neck, before unscrewing the little jar Emma had wrapped in tissues.

'Insomnia's a very normal part of the grieving process,' he explained—only Emma wasn't really listening. She was staring at the white card he had placed on his desk, at the moment of reckoning nearing. She watched him load the pipette, and the arrow she had for so long buried rustled from the leaves. Emma braced herself to face it. 'Sleeping tablets won't necessarily stop the nightmares,' the doctor went on, as two minutes seemed to drag on for ever. 'Would you like me to refer you to a counsellor? Talking things through might help…'

But it was pointless. Emma knew that. Oh, she had nothing against counselling, but there was no point going and them telling a counsellor only half of what was going on in her life.

'Emma…' The shift in his voice made her look up. He wasn't smiling, his face was emotionless and, Emma realised, it would remain that way until he had gauged her reaction. 'You're pregnant.'

'I can't be.'

'You are.' He pushed the little plastic card towards her—the pink cross on it told her she'd failed this test. But even if the evidence was irrefutable, even if at some level she'd already known that she was, still she tried to deny it.

'But I've *had* my period.'

'If you're sure about your dates, then it was probably breakthrough bleeding…that can happen in the first trimester.' Now he smiled—and it was a gentle smile that was kind. 'You *are* pregnant, Emma.'

'I can't be,' she said again, only in an entirely different context. 'I can't possibly be pregnant now.' Not by a man who didn't love her—a man she owed a small fortune to—a man whom, she was fast starting to realise, she mightn't be able to pay him back…

'Emma, accidents happen.' The doctor cut into her pleadings. 'You need some time to get your head around the idea. Now, I want to arrange some blood tests and an ultrasound, just to check your dates, and then we'll schedule an appointment to work out your options.'

She *had* no options.

She could feel the walls closing in, with every exit route blocked—could see his pen scribbling on pads—could hear him, talking about dates and LMPs and foetal sizes. She felt as if she'd suddenly landed in France, with only a schoolgirl guide to aide her, no accommodation booked and just a handful of coins. Completely and woefully unprepared for the journey.

'We'll get those tests done, and I'll see you in the next couple of days. Once we know your dates…'

She didn't hear anything else. Somehow, on autopilot, Emma paid for her consultation and made a follow-up appointment. Then, clutching her referrals, she stepped out into the bright afternoon and, for how long she wasn't sure, sat in the car, staring at the world rushing by at a million miles an hour as for just a little while hers stood still.

She tried to fathom Zarios's reaction—tried to fathom being bound to a man who would want his heir more than he wanted her.

She tried to fathom her own reaction, but that proved just as elusive.

Oh, she'd miss her mum for ever, but never as much as now. Leaning onto the steering wheel, she sobbed as if Lydia had died that very morning. Weeks of grief were no prelude to the pain that ripped through her now. They'd never see, never know, never hold their grandchild... And then her tears stilled. The sign that she'd begged for, pleaded with God for, had come—in the moment when she'd least expected it.

Loneliness lifted as realisation crept in—this little scrap of life, growing inside her now, had been conceived while her parents had still been alive; had been created on the day they had left this earth.

Surely that was no accident?

Sink or swim.

Despite her near drowning, only today did Emma actually understand the meaning of the saying.

Now, when life seemed to be falling apart, it was time to pull it together. There was no rescuer this time, no strong arms to haul her out of the water—she had to make it to shore by herself.

And she would.

If Jake was gambling again—and his avoidance of her attempts to contact him certainly hinted at that—then he wasn't going to pay her back. She'd have to pay Zarios back herself—and then, when she was no longer indebted to him, she'd work out what to do about the baby.

She'd have nothing. A surge of panic gripped her at the prospect, but she deftly knocked it aside. She'd have her baby.

She had talent.

Somehow they'd survive.

Turning on the ignition, Emma took in a steadying

breath, felt the wheel beneath her hands and the pedals beneath her feet, and for the first time since the accident started to take control.

She told herself, even if she didn't quite believe it yet, that she would be okay.

Because—for her baby's sake—she had to be.

'Jake.' Emma saw her brother freeze as he opened the door.

'Now's not a good time, Em. Beth's having a lie-down.' He looked over her shoulder and down the street, but Emma stood her ground.

'I know Beth's gone out.' Brushing past her brother, she walked into his home uninvited. 'I hear your house is on the market. Beth told me you're looking for something with a bigger garden, nearer the city… Oh, and she mentioned you want to take the twins to America, to Disneyland… Sounds expensive, Jake?'

'Beth's always talking things up.'

'You haven't told her, have you?' His silence said everything. 'Mum and Dad's house sale has gone through, the settlement's on Monday—when exactly *are* you going to tell her, Jake?' She could feel her stomach churning as still he didn't answer. 'Or are you not going to?'

'We need a change—a new start. You have no idea what we've been through…'

Instead of pleading he was angry. Instead of begging he was scolding—just as he always did when his back was to the wall. Emma realised for the first time that he blamed everyone but himself for the mess that he was in.

'You're engaged to Zarios D'Amilo. What do you need more money for?'

'It's a loan…' Emma shouted. 'I'm engaged to him till I pay back the loan…'

'Tell him you can't!' Jake shouted louder. 'He won't even notice it—Zarios can afford it.'

'Well, I can't. I lent it you, Jake, you signed an agreement…'

'So sue me,' Jake scoffed.

'I will!' Emma bluffed. 'And I'm going to tell Beth myself what's going on…'

'I'll never see the twins again if you do.' Jake eyeballed his sister. 'And neither will you—Beth's waiting for an excuse, any excuse, to leave. Go ahead,' Jake challenged.

She could hear the twins scampering up the path, Beth's key in the door.

'Tell her.'

'Tell me what?' Beth half smiled, half frowned as she walked in on them. 'Are you two rowing?'

'I'm just telling my sister—' Jake gave a tight smile '—that it would have been nice if she could have called round to tell us about her engagement, instead of us having to read about it in the papers.'

'Oh, leave her alone, Jake! I spoke to her on the phone—I'm sure Emma's got a million things to be getting on with…'

For the first time Beth was actually smiling, and there was lightness to her that, Emma realised, must have come when she'd finally known her marriage was back on track.

'Anyway, she's here now!' Beth picked up Emma's hand and gazed at the ring. 'It's gorgeous…' Beth wrapped her in a hug. 'It's so nice to have some good news at last. Come on, I'll make you a drink—and then I'll bore you senseless about our trip to Disneyland…'

It was at that moment that Emma realised she'd lost close to a million dollars.

'Where have you been?' Zarios asked, when finally she made it home.

'Don't worry, I haven't been kicking up my heels at The Casino…' Exhaustion seeped out of her as with a sigh she sat on the sofa as far away from him as possible. 'I was at my brother's.'

'I'm not checking up on you…I've been worried. You said you were going to the doctor.'

'Which I did.'

'Am I allowed to ask how it went?'

'He asked if I was stressed…' Emma gave an ironic smile. 'I said that I thought I might be.'

'Did he give you anything to help you sleep?'

'No. I have to have some blood tests…' She bent down to take off her sandals. A lousy liar at the best of times, she hoped her fringe would hide her blush. 'So I'm afraid you're going to have to put up with my carry-on for a little while longer. Sorry if I'm disturbing your rest!' she added as she sat up.

'I'm not worried about my rest,' Zarios bristled. 'I'm actually rather worried about you.'

Zarios was seriously worried, in fact.

And he felt seriously guilty, too!

Watching her fade before his eyes, hearing her crying out in the night, made something unfamiliar twist inside him—something that felt suspiciously like guilt. But he had nothing to be guilty for, he had told himself over and over—they had made a deal and she was being handsomely paid for a few weeks' work.

Staring over at her pale features, seeing that once smiling mouth grim now with tension, her head resting back on the sofa, her eyes half closed in exhaustion, he hated the mess she'd got herself into. But he couldn't, just couldn't, hate the woman. Couldn't not put her out of her misery.

'Emma?' She didn't open her eyes as he spoke, which made it somehow easier. 'I'm not going to force you to marry me…and I'm not going to hound you if you can't pay me back. You have helped me enough. The board are pleased—things are going well there. If we can just hold it together for a little while longer then that's enough. I don't want a loveless marriage any more than you do…' He watched as a tear slid out from under her eyelid, and wished he could reach out and touch her— wished it were the middle of night, when he was allowed to hold her. 'My mother didn't love my father—I have no desire to recreate history.'

He was trying to say the right thing, to do as the counsellor had said and take away as much pressure as possible, so why was she crying? Only he didn't have time to dwell. Taking a deep breath, Zarios said the hardest part. 'I rang up some places today—places that deal with addiction…' Now she did open her eyes, those bright blue eyes that had once danced and held his. They were tortured and confused now. 'When this is over, will you think about going…?'

She shot up from her seat, her head buzzing. Jake's cruel words, the doctor's diagnosis, all were just fading into the distance as she stared at the father of her child—

the man who had just admitted he didn't love her, had never intended to marry her.

'You've got it all worked out, haven't you? Ship me off to rehab, why don't you? Even your father will understand then why you had to end it...'

'Emma, please!'

She didn't want to hear it. He shook his head hopelessly, lifted his hand to wipe away a tear. She brushed it off.

'You have a problem...'

'*Jake's* the one with the problem.' She was through lying for her brother—just through with it now.

'Emma....' Wearily Zarios shook his head. 'When will you stop lying? Your father told me your business was going under, and I saw Jake give you money at the party. I spoke with Jake this evening and he confirmed it.'

'You spoke to Jake?!'

'Emma, I'm trying to *help* you.'

'Well, it doesn't feel like it!'

'This might.' He was angry now—angry at her denial, and hurt, too. This was the only woman he had truly put first—the one woman he had, hand on heart, offered to help. The million dollars didn't matter a jot— it was her refusal to acknowledge her problem that incensed him. 'I am flying to Singapore tonight. Hopefully things will be easier on you if I am not around. I'll meet you in Sydney for the ball on Saturday. If we can keep up appearances for a couple more days it would be appreciated. And then I suggest you read the brochures—and *really* think about getting some help.'

'Do you do it deliberately?' Emma asked, furious at the games he played, at how much he must be enjoying setting his trap and watching his victim squirm. 'Do you lie in bed thinking of ways to goad me, to put me down?'

'No...' Zarios didn't bat an eyelid as he stood up. 'I lie in bed at night thinking of you *getting* down...' He walked over to her and ran a finger along her cheek. He put his hand to the back of her head, his fingers knotting in her hair as he stared into her lying eyes, scarcely able to comprehend how much he adored her. 'I lie in bed thinking of you screaming my name. I lie in bed thinking of your legs wrapped around my head as I make you come so hard you beg me to stop.' He lifted her chin with one finger, raising her burning face to look at him. 'But then I remind myself we don't do that sort of thing, because Emma doesn't want to. Which is a shame...'

He dropped contact then, but she could still feel his hand, wished it were still there, wanted it there, wanted him to push her head down so she could kiss the erection that she knew was there waiting, wanted him to make her scream as he had described. She loathed the dignity that held her back as he picked up his suit carrier and headed out of the door. 'It might take your mind off playing the tables.'

The slamming of the door left her reeling, her body as raw, as inflamed, as if they'd just had sex—hot, desperate sex. She headed for the bathroom, lifted her hair and gulped water from the tap. But it did nothing to douse the fire. The cauldron of living with him—of lying in bed and not touching him—she had thought unbearable. But without him...

She'd thought he was trying to goad her. Now she realised he had actually been trying to help her...

She scanned the brochures, reading about the help he

was offering, and the words seemed to leap off the page. She realised that with each denial she had, in his eyes, reinforced that she had a problem. After all, her own brother had told him as much.

Well, what did she expect? Emma thought with a snort of scorn.

But Zarios…

The thought of this incredibly proud man acquiring these, offering to wipe out her debts if only she sought help… Somewhere inside she felt as if she were being stroked. Somewhere in her heart she knew she was glimpsing the real Zarios.

A man who would give anything to help her.

A man who had just admitted how much he wanted her.

A man she wanted, too.

CHAPTER TWELVE

LIVING in fear, Emma realised as she stepped out of the lawyer's office and onto the pavement, was harder than facing it.

Melbourne was delicious this morning, the trees that lined Collins Street giving off a bosky green haze, the heat from the pavement rising through her flimsy sandals, and Emma dipped into a side street café, ordering a large iced chocolate drink and sitting to sip on it, enjoying the simple moment.

Enjoying, for just a little while, the feel in her chest of the absence of fear.

She was doing the right thing.

Oh, any lawyer worth his salt would tell her that, but Emma knew she had been hearing the truth. Knew that, as hard as it might be to execute, the path she had chosen now to follow was the right one.

The only one.

She rolled her eyes at her bleeping phone—Zarios, who hadn't contacted her since he'd left, reminding her that her plane took off at two. As if she didn't already know!

In a few hours she'd see him again.

Only this time with honest eyes.

She would tell him her truth and listen as hopefully he told her his.

'Would you like to see the menu?' a smiling waiter offered, but Emma declined, glancing at her watch and realising she'd better get a move on.

These coming days were without a doubt going to be the biggest, scariest days of her life, but she'd prepared for it. Taking a deep breath, she doused the butterflies that were starting to dance.

It was time to get on with it!

Sydney was much the same as she remembered. The breathtaking view of what was surely the most beautiful harbour in the world matched her mood as the plane glided in.

The roads were as busy, the buildings as big, and the people in as much of a hurry.

And the luxury hotel Zarios was staying in, and where the ball would be held tonight, was as bland and as soulless as his Melbourne home.

She was sick of white bathrobes, Emma thought as she hauled herself out of another sunken bath.

She wanted red, Venetian Red, or Manganese purple—wanted to wrap herself in beach towels that still smelt of the beach and sunscreen, no matter how many times they were laundered!

And for the first time in the longest time she wanted to capture those colours. Wanted to dip her brush in bold primaries—wanted to squeeze out the oiled pigment and craft it into images that breathed and danced into life beneath her fingers.

And she would.

Drying herself with the safe white towel, smiling as her spray tan smeared the bleached cotton, she caught sight of her naked reflection in the vast mirror, for the first time seeing the very real changes that were taking place within her body.

Her breasts were swollen, and the areolae seemed to have doubled in size, and… She frowned down at her stomach. Oh, it was way too early for her to be showing, but there was a softness there, a sort of roundness, that reminded her that this wasn't her secret to keep, that a baby really was growing inside her and that Zarios had every right to know. And somehow, before this weekend was over, she had to find the words to tell him.

Her hands cradled her stomach as she imaged the little life growing in there—filled with love and wonder for the tiny miracle inside her. The fear and grief that had been her companions for so long now were replaced instead by hope—and not just for her baby, but for its parents, too!

She took for ever to get ready. The beautician and hairdresser the hotel had supplied to prepare her did a wondrous job. Tonight she wore her hair piled high on her head, her blue eyes shining bluer thanks to the glittery silver-kissed eyelids that matched her shimmering dress and shoes, while her throat and wrists gleamed with the jewels the sponsor had insisted she wore tonight.

But even when the beautician had gone, even when she stood more groomed and poised than she could ever have imagined, still there was work to be done!

Her shaking hands lit candles, hoping the dimmed lighting would hide her blush, hoping that Zarios wouldn't

roll his eyes at her pathetic attempt at romance and se-
duction.

She placed a hand low on her stomach for reassur-
ance—they had made a baby; there was at least one very
good reason for trying to make this work.

Except as the minutes turned into hours, as the
candles hissed their farewell and drowned in molten
wax, Emma felt more angry than foolish. It had never
entered her head that he mightn't come. Over and
over he had reiterated how important this night was,
but as the hands of the clock crept towards 8:00 p.m.,
Emma realised that Zarios's idea of important differed
widely from hers.

She was tempted not to answer the phone when it rang.

'My flight was delayed.'

'I checked on the Internet.' Emma refused to be lied
to. 'You landed over an hour ago.'

'We did,' Zarios agreed. 'And then unfortunately not
one but two passengers chose to be taken ill, in their
wisdom, and the plane was quarantined until a medical
officer could verify that the cases wasn't related.'

'Oh!'

'Was that a sorry?' Zarios asked.

'No,' Emma said tartly. 'That was a "you could at
least have rung!"'

'I was on another call, trying to appease Tania, the
charity's president…' He grimaced into the phone. 'For
the first time in my life I have a genuine reason for
being late, and no one believes me.'

'That's what an appalling reputation does, I'm afraid.'

He smiled at her tartness. 'Can I ask a favour?'

'No.'

'Can you go ahead without me? I will get changed at the airport as soon as my bags come through…'

'You *are* kidding?'

'No.' Zarios winced. 'There are pre-dinner drinks—Tania said that if you at least can put in an appearance the guests will accept that I am just delayed. I'll be there in half an hour—forty-five minutes at the most.' Pulling out his passport in preparation for Customs, Zarios did a very rare thing. 'Emma, I really am sorry.' He awaited her martyred sigh, frowning when it never came.

Instead came four little words. Only when they were said did he realise how much he'd longed to hear them.

'I missed you, Zarios.'

For the first time since puberty Zarios realised he was blushing. He was standing in the middle of a busy airport and blushing at the sound of her voice, worried he'd misheard, and terrified he might have misinterpreted, but prepared to take the plunge all the same.

'I missed you, too.' He flashed a very male smile at the Customs officer, to show he wasn't really that soft, but, hearing her voice again, he realised that he was.

'Can we talk, Zarios?'

'Please.'

'Properly, I mean.'

'I mean it, too.'

He'd chosen to drive himself to the airport, which with the benefit of hindsight had been stupid. No back of a limousine to dress in. Zarios had to slum it in the first class lounge, cursing like a sailor as he knotted his tie, frantic not that he was late, but to see her.

Every red light chose to greet him. A few Zarios chose to ignore.

Depositing his car, dashing through the foyer, he followed the arrows to the ballroom, consumed with the desire to be beside her. Except everybody wanted a piece of him. Crossing the floor, he felt like a bloody politician as he nodded and waved and stopped to make grating small talk. For now, only from afar could he see her.

She looked stunning. Her hair was blonder, her skin golden, the silver dress she had chosen to wear tonight breathtaking. There was an elusive quality to her that shone even from a distance, and it wasn't just Zarios who could sense it—like moths to a flame she held her audience, and the sound of her laughter was like music to his ears when he finally came up behind her.

She knew he was there—knew even before she felt the heat from his palm on the small of her back—and such was the delight on her face as she turned to greet him that for the first time in his life Zarios felt as if he were home, felt for the first time the simple pleasure of a loving return.

'Ah, my errant fiancé.' Her hand slipped inside his and he held it tightly. 'Glad you finally made it.'

'We hardly noticed you weren't here…' Even Tania, the president of the charity, appeared mollified by Emma's charms. 'Zarios.' She snapped into business mode. 'We ought to head over to the Governor.'

God, but he earned his stripes that night.

Chatting, laughing, drinking, eating—and yet all the while just wanting her, wanting the crowd to thin, resisting the urge to just grab her hand and take her up to their suite. But there was some sweet relief. When the endless dinner was over, when his speech had been executed, finally he could relax. Could wrap his arms around her on the dance floor and hold her again.

As they danced, as he held her as he had that first night, he was catapulted back to when it had been just the two of them, when it was about laughter and fun and fancy, being bound together for no other reason than that was where they wanted to be. So many nights he had wanted to call her, to apologise for his harsh words on leaving, to offer his help again—and he would do that, Zarios decided. Just not now. Not in a room where everyone was watching. For now he would just have to make do with the pleasurable option of holding her.

'If we had met for the first time tonight...' Zarios stared down at her '...if this was our first dance, what would you be thinking?'

'That I wish the night could go on for ever.'

'Anything else?' Zarios asked.

There were so many things she could have said, but in that slice of time there was only one thing she wanted. 'That I wish you would kiss me.'

That he *could* make happen.

Life was, Emma realised as his lips met hers, a series of kisses—some that mattered and some that couldn't be recalled. A mish-mash of hellos and goodbyes, of greeting and farewell, but sometimes, like this time, it was about existing.

This delicious human ritual, the blending of flesh, the sweet poignancy of sharing, was surely the part that mattered the most, which made one human—because only a kiss could truly forgive, and this kiss did that.

One kiss—the sustenance they needed to make it through the night—and then, much, much later, another kiss as they stood in the cool midnight air outside the hotel, waiting for the valet service to retrieve his car.

'Why aren't we going up to your room?' Emma grumbled. All night she had wanted to be alone with him, all night they had been aching to get away, and now that they had, now that their bed awaited, Zarios had moved the carrot.

'Because I want to take you home.'

As the car purred away from the city, through the hilly Sydney streets, she could never have guessed at his nervousness. Gates parted and the car slid into a garage, and as they stepped out Emma found that she was frowning, unsure as to why Zarios had selected a key and opened a front door.

It was the normality of it, Emma realised as she stepped inside. The normality of a key on a ring and Zarios letting himself in had momentarily dazed her—and never more than now, as she walked through the hall and into the lounge.

Oh, there was no doubt it was a luxurious property—the view alone took care of that, the ocean seeming almost touchable from the clifftop vantage point—but it wasn't even that that had her breath catching in her throat. It was the telescope set up beside the window, the low comfortable cushions, a book turned pages-down on the coffee table.

Zarios had been right.

This was a home.

'I don't get here often enough.' Zarios was flicking on lights, shrugging off his jacket, and instead of contemptuously tossing it on the floor for someone else to pick up, he actually hung it—if not on a hanger in the wardrobe, at least over the back of a chair.

'Progress!' Emma commented.

'Sorry?'

'If you keep practising, in a couple of days you might even manage to hang up a towel.'

'I only have someone come in once a week here— to stock up the fridge and keep the place ready for me. If I don't put it away myself…' He actually smiled as it dawned on him she was being sarcastic, and Emma found she was doing the same. Especially when he offered her coffee and actually made it himself.

'The view's stunning.'

The moon was waxing, just a couple of nights away from being full, and it lit up the inky water, catching the surf and highlighting it as it crashed to the beach. Zarios had slid open one of the vast windows, the Pacific Ocean was roaring its tune, and Emma realised that she was nervous. For days she'd waited for this moment, but now that it was actually here she wondered how to approach it—almost yearned for the anonymity of a hotel room, for the vagabond existence she had thought was his. Because here amongst his things, here in his home, Emma felt wrong-footed, embarrassed, almost, at her presumption that there was something she could offer him.

If Zarios wanted a family, then surely he would already have had one?

'Excuse me a moment…' she said, and she dashed to the bathroom.

There was a run in her very sheer stockings and Emma pulled them off. It was a relief to get out of her

Magic Knickers, too, to gulp some water from the tap, and then glance around at his things.

Zarios's things.

No glass bottles, no matter how fancy, filled from the vats belonging to a hotel, but *his* things. Cologne and shaving brushes... Funny that a box of cotton buds could make her smile, or thick brown towels and a book by the bath, which must have been dropped in it at one point because the pages were all wrinkled.

She tried to picture the room with baby lotions and nappies and a bath full of toys, but she couldn't. The heir he seemingly desired was a person in its own right, not a Band Aid to hold two people together.

She wished she could stop the clock, could pause the changes in her body long enough for them to work it out, long enough to establish the couple before the family.

Which was what she wanted to do tonight.

She'd put on weight.

Zarios watched her as she crossed the lounge room. Oh, he knew women too well to comment—knew she wouldn't believe him even if he insisted that he liked what he saw.

And he *did* like it.

Her legs were bare now, and still slender, but there was a roundness to her hips that suited her, and her breasts... Zarios found his tongue was on the roof of his mouth as he saw the swell of them, the sheer silver fabric accentuating swollen nipples.

There were so many reasons for her not to walk over to him—they needed to talk, needed to sort things out— except they needed togetherness more. It was as if some invisible thread were pulling her. The memory of his kiss was still alive on her mouth, and if somehow she could capture that, if somehow they could retrieve the closeness they had once shared, surely then they would be in a better position to sort things out?

Always he was beautiful—that was never in question—only tonight he was exquisitely so. His jacket was off, his tie loosened, his jaw dark, his cheekbones savage in the dim light and his dark eyes quietly watching. She wanted to bound up to him like a crazy puppy, or jump on his knee like a purring kitten, but instead she walked over.

'Come here.' He made the last few steps easy, caught her wrist and pulled her onto his knee. 'Come here so I can never let you go again,' he said. And if it was just about sex, if it was just about lust, why did he hold her for a full moment before kissing her? He pressed his face in her hair, as if her scent was enough, but only for a moment before the tension, the want that had simmered, eternally checked, infinitely controlled, was let loose in one savage motion—the hungry search for each other's mouth.

Greedy, greedy kisses that at first had nothing to do with pleasing the other, just satisfying one's hungry self—tasting, licking, sucking and confirming the other was real. His kisses were so potent, yet so desperate as mouths still entwined, he spun her round on his lap so she was straddling him. There was no choice but to hitch up her dress to accommodate his thighs between hers. His fingers grazed the bare flesh of her upper thighs, and she felt his low moan in her mouth as his fingers slid higher.

'Oh, Emma…' His hands cupped her bottom. 'You should have told me…'

A shocked gurgle of laughter filled her throat that he thought she had been walking around all night with no panties—but why spoil it when she was sliding down his zipper, freeing his delicious erection? She felt almost sick with want. His fingers were working her zipper also, his hands creeping in at the sides of her dress, the pad of his thumb working a nipple—till it wasn't enough, either for her or him. He broke the strap on her dress with mutual consent and then, capturing her breast in his mouth, sucked greedily as she pressed his length against her heat.

He lifted her buttocks the generous inches it would take to accommodate him, his mouth still working her breast, then came the heaven of him entering her. She could see him, sliding deep inside her, and it was the most erotic thing she had ever seen—his endless length teasing her, his hands moving her up and down more slowly than she would have preferred. But even if she was on top, it was Zarios who was in control.

'All the nights I have wanted you…'

'I wanted you, too…'

She was giddy with want, fighting his strong hands, wanting to move faster. But he wouldn't relent, each measured stroke deep inside coveting her, revealing the beauty of gleaming black hair against soft blonde curls. And still, even as she came, still he moved her slowly, wouldn't let her orgasm abate. He just ground her hips down to meet his, over and over again, till her body imploded, till she screamed out his name, till she was coming again. Only then did he let her move with wild abandon as he pulsed deep inside her, taking her closer to the edge than it was surely safe to do, then pulling her back when she was sure she was lost for ever.

'I missed you…' Still his kisses were urgent as he carried her to his bed a mesh of arms and legs, and she lay drunk on a cocktail of sensations. His slow deep kisses breathed life back into her and she kissed him again. It could never be so good with anyone but him. It was as though he could see inside her, could read her as if he *was* her.

'Can we make it?' Black eyes stared down at her. 'Could you forget the hurt, forget the past…?'

'Can you?'

'Yes.'

Oh, but it was too simple an answer—and her resolve to establish *them* before she brought in the rest of world faded with the caress of his eyes.

'Zarios, when I accepted the loan I thought there would be no problem. I mean…' Her mouth was impossibly dry. She was scared to trust him with her brother's secret, but scared not to. Scared not just because of the debt that would go unpaid, but scared for the future— because Jake was hurtling head-first into a pit of no return. Her parents were gone, and when her brother didn't pay her back their relationship would be gone, too. 'I wasn't honest with you when I asked for the loan…'

'It doesn't matter.' He shooed it away. But for Emma it did matter.

'It does…'

'It's money…' he kissed her mouth '…of which I have plenty. Forget about it.'

His mouth was toying with hers, numbing her panic, and when he kissed her like this she could kiss him for ever—because here in his bed, here in his arms, it was about so much more than a debt unpaid.

'I need your help.'

'You have it.' His tongue slid into her lips. 'Tomorrow we will sort out whatever trouble you are in. But tonight…'

Tonight was theirs. Tonight was about making love over and over, about lying in his arms afterwards and glimpsing a future she'd never dared to. A cot in the corner, their baby in bed beside them…

Sweet dreams were her visitors that night.

CHAPTER THIRTEEN

COULD they make it?

Walking in the surf, wearing one of his shirts and a rolled-up pair of his shorts, feeling the whip of water on her ankles, the salty spray on her face, her body deliciously tender from his attention, Emma relished the time alone as she tried to sensibly ask the question.

Yes!

Despite the damning evidence to the contrary, despite the appalling reputation that preceded him, somehow she knew he was better than that. That it wasn't a baby that would be holding them together when she summoned the strength to tell him—instead it was the love they'd shared last night that would bind them.

Climbing onto soft sandstone rocks, she hugged her knees as she gazed out, watched the early-morning swimmers race in the ocean pool, and shivered at the very thought. Yet there was no sight more beautiful than Coogee in the morning. Surfers waiting patiently in the distance for the wave that would carry them to the shore, lone joggers getting their fix of nature before they headed to their offices and computers.

All this she could have.

All this their child could have.

She could almost picture it—a child as blonde as herself or as dark as Zarios, laughing, running…

And Emma stilled.

Only her eyes moved—scanning, processing the colourful scene before her and trying to condense it into a grainy snapshot.

The same snapshot she had seen at Rocco's.

Of the slice of time when Zarios had been happy.

Craning her neck, she stared up at his windows, pondered the demons that haunted him, this most difficult and complicated man.

And vowed that together they'd face them.

The raised voices that greeted her as she pushed open the front door had her hesitating. The thick throaty sobs of a woman crying had every one of her hackles up. Miranda, perhaps—or another ex-lover come to plead for a second chance? All these thoughts whirred through her mind as she walked through the hallway.

All were laid to rest before she even got to the lounge.

Rapid words were being fired in Italian by Zarios.

The throaty sobs of their recipient told Emma they were brutal.

'Per favore…'

She was as beautiful as her son, her black eyes desperate, pleading with him to just listen, but Zarios was having none of it.

'Fuori!' He shooed her away as if she were a gypsy come begging, and when that didn't work, when she grabbed at his arm, he dusted her off as if she were some filthy fly. 'Out!' He bundled her bag in her

arms, dismissing her so absolutely that Emma felt her blood run cold.

'Zarios…' She was torn, wanting to go after his mother but desperate to talk sense to him. 'She's your *mother*!'

'Mother?' He spat the word out. '*Puttana*, more like. Now she is back—now, when my father is near his grave, she decides she loves him, decides she made a mistake. It is thirty years too late…'

'For who?' Emma pleaded. 'It's not too late for your father—he never stopped loving her.'

'Then he's a fool!' Zarios snarled. 'All she wants is his money. It's all *any* of you want—' He stopped talking then, halted himself mid-sentence. But it was too late, the words were already out, his poison free. And she tasted it, glimpsed a future that was only as good as his most recent apology.

'I'll pay you back.' Oh, she would—she'd rather lose everything to Jake than be indebted to Zarios. 'On Monday you'll get every cent back.'

'Don't bother.' He stared right at her as he flung the final knife. 'We agreed that if I was unfaithful then you didn't owe me anything.' It hit her right between the eyes—the pain, the humiliation, all repeated—and she hated, loathed herself that she had let him do it to her again.

'You bastard.'

'Nothing's changed, then.' Zarios gave her a black smile. 'Go on—off you go…'

'Just like that.' She couldn't believe the callousness of him—that after all they'd shared last night he could so easily eradicate her, could loathe her so readily when so recently he'd adored her. 'Zarios, what about your father? The board?'

'I don't care!' Zarios roared. 'I don't care what they think any more. *I* am the one who made them rich—I am the one who lined their greedy palms. If they think they are better off without me then let them try.'

'You don't care about anyone.' She was scooping her stuff into a handbag, desperate to just get the hell out. 'You're so busy looking for the worst in people—'

'Where's the good?' Zarios interrupted. 'Tell me, where *is* the good?'

'I loved you!' Words that should had been said gently were instead hurled. 'I loved you right from that first night—but finally you've succeeded in convincing me that I was a fool.'

But fools still had feelings, fools still glimpsed paradise—and last night she had.

And she'd have given anything to reclaim it.

'I'm pregnant, Zarios.' She was trembling, shaking as she said it—hoping, praying, the words would slam some sense into him, would halt the row long enough so that they could at least talk. But he was unreachable.

For Zarios it was as if he were staring at Miranda, as if he were having his skull split with an axe. He had braced himself to be felled two weeks ago—he had never expected it today. Her last frantic attempts to salvage the situation made him sick to the stomach. So sick, he couldn't even look at her, struggling to even utter a single word.

'So?'

It was the cruellest of responses, and on behalf of their child she hated him for it. Yet there was a quiet dignity to her as she countered his poison.

'I'm letting you know just so you can't say I didn't tell you.'

'Put it in a letter from your lawyer.' Zarios shrugged. 'That's it?'

'Send me the bill…' Zarios jeered. 'But for now—get the hell out. You make me sick, just looking at you.'

He even had the gall to offer her his driver, but pale, nauseous, she declined, unable to even look at him, too numb even to be stunned at his sheer callousness.

'It's okay…'

She must have looked like a madwoman—dressed in his clothes, with bare feet and a sparkly handbag, and talking to herself.

Except she wasn't talking to herself. She was talking to their child.

Her child.

'We're going to be just fine, little one.'

Waving down a taxi, Emma asked to be taken to the hotel, then told the driver to wait as she grabbed her things, then headed to the airport.

It was *her* baby now, and Zarios could take her to court to prove otherwise.

He'd have to fight for the right to call it his now—he'd lost that privilege an hour ago.

CHAPTER FOURTEEN

'DOVE?' Incensed, furious, Rocco pounced on his son, demanding to know where he'd been. Thoroughly untogether, and reeking of brandy fumes, Zarios was present if not correct for the board meeting on Monday morning. '*Dove siete stato?*'

'Enjoying the fruits of my labour.' Zarios stared at his father. 'I work hard, so I play hard.'

'The paper says your engagement is over—'

'You believe the papers?' Zarios shrugged.

'You were to behave!' Rocco roared. 'All I asked was that for a couple of months you pulled your head in—instead you shame me. Engaged one minute, broken off the next—and what about Emma?'

'You were the one who warned me off her!' Zarios pointed out.

But Rocco refused to back down. He was so incensed he could hardly get the words out. 'Because I knew what you'd do! And now—now when my life's work is to be decided—you arrive *ubriaco*—'

'I am not drunk,' Zarios interrupted. 'I wish I *were* drunk—it would be easier to face those buffoons. Instead I will do it with a hangover! *You* should be the one doing this—you should be reminding them that *you* built this company, that this has been your life, this is what you chose over raising your child. And yet you let them walk all over you.'

'I will not be here soon. I am trying to make sure they accept you as their leader—that things—'

'Lead, then!' Zarios said. 'Lead me into the boardroom now and they can make their choice. But I will tell them what I am now telling you—I will *never* serve to appease!'

The blinds hadn't even been opened in the board-room. Unshaven, dishevelled, and with bags under his eyes so heavy they looked like bruises, Zarios faced those who considered themselves his peers and smiled darkly at them.

'My father founded this company forty years ago—here in Melbourne. Now it is multinational, now it is a world leader—and now, when my father is due to retire, you question whether its name should remain D'Amilo. Now you question the leadership of the family that has enriched your lifestyle. There is no question.'

Zarios snapped open the blinds, drenching the board-room in sunlight, and, despite his dishevelled state, somehow he was the most dignified of all of them.

'With the massive returns last year, while you were adding to your retirement fund or purchasing your beachside home, I, too, was securing my future.' He jabbed a finger at the office block beyond. 'In every D'Amilo boardroom around the world, if you look out of the window the view will be the same: I have secured prime office space in every city where this company trades, and I am telling you now that I can and I will take my family name and start again. And I will succeed—

because that is what the D'Amilo name means.' He eye-balled every one of his colleagues. 'You are either be-hind me one hundred percent, or you can sit at your desks and wave to me from this window.'

He didn't even wait for their response—just stalked out of the boardroom and back to his luxurious office, telling his assistant he was not to be disturbed under any circum-stances. Flicking off the lights, he lay on his leather sofa and tried to turn off his thoughts, tried not to go down *that* path. But at every turn the map led the same way, her face was the only thing he could picture. The only solace was sleep—at least in his dreams she was laughing.

'They are behind you.'

'Of course they are.' Zarios had shaved and changed, his hair was gleaming. He was utterly together.

'You are right.' For the first time ever Rocco praised his son. 'I am proud of you.'

'I will not let your company down.' Zarios accepted his compliment with backhanded grace. 'I may let my-self down at times, but it will never translate to our shareholders.'

'Your mother is coming back to me.'

As Zarios opened his mouth to tell his father exactly what he thought of that decision the older man got there first.

'Thirty years later in life than you, my son, I have worked out that I don't care what others think any more. Just as you will not appease them—I will not appease you. I love your mother. I have missed her for half of my life…'

'Can't you see she is just back now you are ill—now there is money?'

'Perhaps...' Rocco shrugged—the same shrug he had inadvertently handed down to his son. 'But is it better to die cold and alone in bed with your pride intact, or warm and caressed and believing that love exists?'

'What if she *is* using you, Pa?' They both knew Zarios wasn't talking about his mother as for the first time he begged his father's advice. 'What if you *know* she is trouble? What if you *know*?'

'Then you ask yourself if the good outweighs the bad.'

Oh, and it did. Closing his eyes, Zarios recalled Emma's scent, the sound of her laughter, and knew that he would lie for a week in the gutter with banshees wailing over him if it meant he could spend one night by her side.

'People don't have to be perfect for us to love them,' Rocco said. 'Emma is proof of that.'

'Emma?' Zarios frowned; they were supposed to be talking about *him*.

'You're the buffoon.' Rocco smiled. 'When will you get it in your head that Emma loves you?'

He would tell her.

Sitting at his desk, Zarios rested his head in his hands, his fingers bunching in his cropped hair as he prepared himself for the hardest task—to trust her, to forgive her, to tell her he was sorry.

He didn't care about the money, and he could help her with her problems—because what they had found, what they had shared, albeit briefly, was priceless.

'Zarios!' Jake knocked on his office door, his smile wide. 'Have you seen Beth or Emma? We were supposed to be meeting in the coffee bar opposite before coming to sign all the papers and tidy everything up.'

'Not yet…' Zarios dragged himself from his intro-spection and forced a smile, then glanced at his watch. 'There's still a while yet.'

'I can't get hold of Beth, that's all—maybe she's having trouble with the babysitter.'

'Maybe.' Zarios shrugged, because talk of babysit-ters and the like was a foreign language to him. 'Jake, I wanted to talk to you. When I rang you the other day about Emma—'

'Actually—' Jake gave a tiny grimace '—when we discussed Emma's problem—well, I didn't feel com-fortable anyway. But given you were practically fam-ily…' He dropped the apologetic smile. 'And now you're not.'

'I still have your sister's best interests at heart.'

'Really?' Jake frowned in distaste. 'I think it would be better for everyone if you kept your distance.'

Which made sense, Zarios told himself. After all, Jake was just looking out for his sister—but he hadn't seemed too concerned moments before.

An uneasy feeling was building inside Zarios. Emma had said Jake was the one with the problem, and he'd dismissed it as her being in denial. Jake with the beam-ing smile and gleaming shoes. Jake with his fancy car and nice city lifestyle.

Jake with the depressed wife and out-of-control twins.
Damn.

His mind was racing, he was dialling her number, leaving rambling messages on her message bank. He at-tempted to filter their every conversation, trying to discard, dismiss, verify, trying to assimilate the facts…

Charging out of his office, he was just in time to

glimpse the meeting room door close, Zarios rueing the fact he'd removed himself from the management of their parents' estate. Pacing the floor like a caged animal, he wanted to be in there, wanted to be on the other side of the door, sitting beside Emma.

Emma halted her own pacing for a second and stared at her bleeping phone. There had been several frantic messages from Jake, asking where she was, and now Zarios had joined in—ringing her, texting her. Well, they'd all know soon enough.

'Thanks for coming…' Emma felt like the biggest bitch in the world as she let Beth into her tiny flat. 'Where are the twins?'

'I'm having them looked after today.' Shy, evasive, Beth declined a drink and then perched on the edge of Emma's sofa. 'You know, don't you?'

'Know?'

'That I'm leaving him today.'

Emma felt the thud as the rest of her world crashed.

'I'm not after his money.' Beth shook her head. 'He can have it—he can go throw it up the wall or put it on black—I just don't care any more…'

And Emma saw it then. If *she* had danced on the edge of Jake's addiction then Beth had lived in the full clutch of it. Here was a woman who was ready to walk away with nothing more than the clothes she was wearing and her babies—who deserved so much more.

'I love your brother…' Her tired, puffy eyes met Emma's. 'But as much as I love him I hate him. I know there isn't a good time to leave. I've tried…' great sobs heaved at her body '…but there was always something to get past first—the twins' birthday, Christmas, your dad's sixtieth, your parents' funeral—I keep waiting for the moment to be right. And it's not coming. Today,' she sobbed, 'he gets a million dollars. Please, God, today I can go…'

There was nothing she couldn't tell this woman, Emma realised as she put her arms around tired, weary shoulders—nothing she could say that would hurt her more than she already was.

'I know.' She felt tension, denial in her sister-in-law's shoulders. 'I know how hard this has been on you, and I'll do what I can for you and the twins. Beth…' She felt the mingling of grief and relief flood through her sister-in-law as she offered her support. 'I know about his habit. I've lent him my share of the inheritance…'

'More fool you, then.' Beth's voice was bitter, but Emma knew it wasn't aimed at her. 'You know you won't get it back?'

'I've hired a lawyer.' Emma's voice was shaking as she admitted to her sister-in-law what she had done. 'He's representing me today—Jake's just about to find out.'

As Jake marched out, his face like thunder, Zarios knew his hunch had been right. The nice-guy act had vanished and, not even acknowledging Zarios, he brushed past, banging his hand on the lift button, impatience in every cell. He finally gave in and took the stairs.

'You did the right thing!' Jed, one of the directors, rolled his eyes as the exit door slammed. 'Removing yourself—I don't think I've ever seen a nastier hand-over of assets.'

But Zarios wasn't listening. His eyes were looking over his colleagues' shoulder as the members of the meeting tripped out, desperate to see her, to offer his late support.

'Where's Emma?'

'She sent a lawyer on her behalf. The transaction went ahead, and then Jake was served with notice. She's suing him for the money he owes her, and all his assets have been frozen. He owes money everywhere.' Jed's lips were grim. 'Can't help but feel sorry for him, really. Not only did his pay-day not come, he's just found out that his wife's left him, too.'

Zarios could feel the blood pounding in his temples as realisation struck. The problem he had brushed aside when she'd tried to tell him, so sure had he been that the debt had been hers, had been her trying to help her brother. Ice seemed to be running through his veins and yet he was sweating, Zarios realised, as he recalled Jake's murderous expression as he left the office.

A man at rock bottom was a dangerous one.

'It's not his fault, of course…' Irony laced Jed's words. 'We're trying to contact the wife to warn her…'

But he was speaking to an empty space. Zarios was two steps ahead, jumping into the lift that had appeared, desperate to get to Emma—to warn her, to tell her, to protect her.

He could taste bile in his throat, the bitter, acrid taste of fear, and it was swirling in his stomach and rising as full realisation hit.

She had been telling the truth—and not just about her brother.

He ground the gears on his car as he wove through

clogged, grid-locked traffic, his mind frantic. He had to get there!

Zarios gave up on the car, depositing it in the middle of the street as angry commuters furiously sat on their horns. But he was running so fast, the blood so loud in his temples, he didn't even hear them. He had to get there—to protect not just the woman he loved, but the mother of his child.

'Open the door!' Emma could hear the door being pounded. 'You bitch, Emma. Open the door!'

'You didn't lock it…' Beth's eyes were frantic as her husband demanded to be let in.

'Go and hide in the bedroom,' Emma urged. 'I'll go.' Creeping down the steps, ready to turn the lock, she wasn't scared. She knew in her heart of hearts that Jake wouldn't hurt her, that he was angry, raging, but would never hurt her.

And then she missed a step.

The fall happened as the door flew open, and piercing pain shot through her before she even hit the ground. The anger in her brother's eyes faded into terror as he stared down at her.

There was the strangest sense of déjà vu as she awoke.

Zarios was sitting in the chair beside her bed, and her body was racked with a piercing sense of loss that she dared not explore.

'You're okay…' In a second he was beside her.

'The baby…' Her hands moved to her stomach, trying to fathom change.

'We'll know soon.'

His hot hand found hers as her lips and eyes moved downwards in a spasm of pain at the helplessness of it all. Her face crumpled as she remembered what had happened.

'Jake?'

'Don't worry about Jake.'

'Oh, but I do…'

'I know.'

'He didn't hit me.'

'I know,' Zarios said again.

'He wouldn't have—'

'Yes, Emma, he *would* have,' Zarios cut in then, clutching her hand gently as he made her face the unpalatable truth. 'He's already pushed Beth, and he *would* have hit you. That's what terrified him the most—the things that made him finally admit he had to get help. When he realised that he could have hit a pregnant woman—could have been responsible for the loss of your baby… You fell trying to lock your door on him. You have to stop making excuses for him, Emma.'

'He's my brother.'

'I never said you had to stop loving him.'

He was right. That much she had already decided for herself. Talking to the lawyer, choosing to take back control, to refuse to be manipulated, to own what was hers…none of it meant that she didn't love him.

'Where is he?'

'At a clinic.'

Zarios held her hand as if he was imparting bad news, but all Emma could feel was the flood of relief, and years of anxiety, of worry, of fear, lifted as Zarios uttered the words she had fought against yet longed to hear.

'It's for three months minimum—he agreed to go.'

'Rehab?'

'He will get rehab eventually, but for now they are dealing with his depression. Then he will get all the help he so desperately needs. It's a top centre. I have guaranteed…' He didn't finish. Somehow they both knew that it didn't matter—that this wasn't and never had been nor could be about money.

'How's Beth?'

'Beth is at my home in Sydney with her mother and the twins. She wanted to stay to see that you were well, but I wanted her out of the way while I dealt with Jake. She is very tired and she needs to rest. She has carried so much…'

'The baby…' she said again. She cared about Beth, but she cared about her baby more. Not a single thing could hold her attention till she knew the answer.

'Don't distress yourself.' He attempted to soothe her. 'You must rest. The doctor says you must not get upset. You'll be having an ultrasound soon, and we'll find out how our—'

She turned her head to face him. '*Our?* How come it's *our* baby suddenly?'

'I'm sorry, Emma. Sorry for not believing you…sorry for the terrible things I said. Sorry for the stupidity that made me nearly lose you both. When I saw Jake charging off for the first time in my life I tasted fear. I realised that I loved you.'

'No.' She shook her head on the pillow. 'I don't want to hear you say that you love me. Now, when you find out that I have been telling the truth, that I *am* having a baby, that I'm actually a decent person, you suddenly decide that you've loved me all along.'

'No!'

He had always been brutal in his honesty, so why, Emma reasoned, should she expect any less now?

'I have been doing my level best not to trust you and certainly to never love you—I didn't admit it to myself till today at one-forty-two p.m. For the first time in my life I listened to my father, and I realised that maybe being in love with a compulsive gambler, a self-confessed gold-digger, who had *told* me that she only wanted me for what I could give her, maybe wouldn't be so bad if at the end of each and every day I got to hold her.'

'I can never trust you.' Emma shook her head at the hopelessness of it.

It was too late.

'Never?' Zarios checked, and resolutely she nodded. 'Even if I told you that since that morning on the beach, since the first time we made love, I have not slept with another woman?'

'Please!' Emma managed a thin laugh.

'We'll need you to excuse us now!' A bossy, old-school nurse popped her head around the door.

She was the first woman Zarios had met who was impervious to his charms—because very clearly she told him that, no, he couldn't have five more minutes, that Ms Hayes was due in ultrasound soon, and after that needed her rest.

'Maybe just till the porter arrives?' It was Emma who asked—Emma who was told that she had two minutes, and that if she needed anything—the elderly nurse shot Zarios a venomous look—she was to ring the bell.

'You went back to Miranda—do you really expect me to believe you didn't sleep with her?'

'When I left you that morning I was fully intending to begin a relationship with you. I couldn't wait for the christening to be over so that I could call you. Miranda was waiting for me, though. She told me she was pregnant…' He frowned, as if just realising how very careless they had been that day. 'Until that morning with you I had always been careful, but I knew these things happened…'

'I thought she couldn't have children?'

'I don't know if she can…'

His voice was a whisper, a croak, his words confusing her. She opened her mouth to argue, to tell him she was tired of his lies, but she recoiled at what she saw. Zarios, who was always so together, always so ahead of the game, looked utterly destroyed. Grief was stamped on his face, and his mouth opening on words that wouldn't come out.

As the porter swished into the room with the trolley that would take her for the ultrasound it was Emma who asked again for one more moment—Emma who just didn't *get* what he was trying to say.

The door closed, and Emma knew that she had to listen without interruption. She wanted to rattle him, to shake him, for him to just *tell* her—except she had never seen a face so haunted with pain, and knew she couldn't rush him now.

'I was stunned…' Zarios shook his head as he relived it. 'I was thinking of you—of seeing you again on Monday—and suddenly Miranda was telling me she was pregnant, and that we must keep it quiet as she had some big work coming up. I was disappointed for you and me—for us.' His black eyes met hers. 'But I told myself that it had been one day, one night… I could not weigh that against a baby.'

She nodded—because that much she *could* get. 'Did you feel trapped?'

'No.' Zarios's answer seemed to surprise him as much as it did her. 'Emma, my mother left us because *she* felt trapped—she felt she was not a good enough mother and that I was better off without her. No matter her reasons, she was wrong. A poor parent is still that child's parent. I always promised myself that I would never do to my child what was done to me. I had never considered having a baby, yet when the idea presented itself I was happy. I was determined to do my best, to build a home… I fell in love with that baby within a minute of Miranda telling me.

'But we did not sleep together. I was still unsure—not about the baby, but about her. I told her I was worried that sex might affect the baby—a stupid excuse. She flew to Brazil for her photo-shoot and I joined her. But she wasn't taking care of herself. I arrived unannounced. She was drinking and smoking when I got there, taking laxatives—all the stuff she did to stay thin, all the stuff that drove me crazy when we were together. We argued.'

'I can see why,' Emma admitted.

'She accused me of being old-fashioned, of trying to police her…which I guess I was. When we came back to Melbourne I asked her to come here, where I have now brought you, to see the top specialist. She insisted on seeing her own doctor. She kept on trying to sleep with me, but I was angry. I wanted to be sure that the baby was okay. And then—' He started to run his hand through his hair then stopped, screwing his fingers so tightly together it must surely have hurt. 'I had never seen a scan—she had never let me come with her to the doctor. Finally, after an argument, she agreed to come here. I drove her and she kept the lie going right to the receptionist's desk.' His eyes were two deep pools of pain. 'There never was a baby. It was to get us back together. She was hoping she would quickly fall pregnant…'

'She never even was…?' Emma couldn't keep the shock from her voice.

'Which meant there was nothing to be upset about—nothing to grieve. Because it had never existed. Nothing had been lost. I was just a fool who for a little while had believed…'

'You're not a fool, Zarios.'

'I *loved* that baby.'

It was hard for men—that much Emma could see. Her body was a melting pot of hormones, of changes not yet visible, but her pregnancy was real just the same. All Zarios had had was Miranda's word—a word he had believed. And just as Emma loved her baby, just as she would move the world to make it right for the little life inside her, he had loved his, too.

Even if it had never existed.

'I'm sorry.' It wasn't her mistake, it wasn't her lie, but she truly *was* sorry. 'It must have been hell.'

'I found out there was no baby the week before you came to see me at my office to ask me for money. And when you told me that *you* were pregnant…' Zarios closed his eyes '…it felt as if it was happening again.'

'This one's real!' She tried to smile, tried to be brave—but what if she was wrong? What if it was already too late?

'I know.' He held her hand. 'And, whatever the outcome, this little one is loved.'

There was no delaying the porter this time. Emma climbed over onto the trolley, trying to fathom the mind of a woman who would lie like that—and trying to fathom Zarios's pain at being told that the little life wasn't just over, but had never even existed in the first place.

'Can he come with me?'

The bossy nurse was actually very kind. 'What do *you* want, Ms Hayes? Of course it's in all the papers that your relationship is over—and I don't want any of my patients feeling pressured…'

'I think I'd like him to come with me.' Emma swallowed, terrified of the outcome, but knowing now that Zarios was just as scared, too.

'Just some cold jelly on your stomach.'

It was routine to the sonographor. Oh, she was kind, but she was efficient and just a little bit distant—maybe she had to be? Emma thought. Having to regularly face parents whose dreams had been dashed.

'I want this baby,' Emma said, because it was imperative that she voiced it, that this little scrap inside her knew that it was wanted and loved.

'I know.' Zarios's hand was over hers.

'Do you want me to turn the screen away?' the sonographor offered, but Emma shook her head, feeling the probe move over her stomach, watching great black and white shapes swoop and swirl on the screen, clouds dashing in and out of focus, like travelling at speed through a tunnel.

And suddenly there it was….

Floating in its little universe, safe and unperturbed by the drama that had taken place, its whole chest a heart-beat that pumped and moved, their baby swung as if on some invisible trapeze, whooping and wriggling and very much alive.

'About ten and a half weeks…' the sonographor said, clicking away. 'Too early to tell the sex at this stage.'

'It doesn't matter.' Zarios spoke when Emma couldn't.

'I'll print off some photos.'

Those were the sweetest words she had ever heard.

Rest and more rest were the doctor's orders.

A slightly irritable uterus, a bruised lower back and an emotionally exhausted mother—there was nothing else he could prescribe.

Sitting in Zarios's car, pale, shaken, clutching her photo, Emma stared at a world that seemed just a bit brighter somehow. All the dirty secrets were out in the open now, and the world was a better place for it.

Jake was getting the help he needed and her baby was alive.

Closing her eyes, she rested against the passenger window, locked in a twilight world between waking and sleep, vaguely aware that the car-ride was taking ages, but too sleepy to question why.

She was imagining herself on the beach road, but in control now—her parents were riding safely along with her, no crumbling cliffs or murky waters, just the shriek of gulls and the delicious salty fragrance of her home…

The car door opened.

'We're here.'

She blinked, seeing her home, her family home, for the first time since the funeral.

And she wasn't so much in shock as he helped her up the stairs and into her familiar bedroom as simply at peace. There were no more questions.

The answers could wait till later.

She could hear banging, but she ignored it. Later— ages later—she was woken with grapefruit juice and toast by an unshaven, tatty-jeaned, strangely calm playboy, who stretched out on her single bed, watching her from its foot, his head on his hands, smiling as he watched her eat.

'You look better.'

'Thank you, Doctor.'

'You do.' He smiled over to her. 'However, I have taken an executive decision and told my parents that you are not up to receiving visitors just yet.'

She didn't say anything—scared she'd misheard, scared she might rush in on what was such a sensitive area—but Zarios was still smiling, a lovely self-mocking smile that quenched her thirst as much as the grapefruit juice did.

'At thirty-four years of age I now have a mother who thinks she can tell me what I should be doing—I am to feed you soup, apparently.'

'Sounds nice.'

'And we are not to have sex till the baby is here.'

'We'll listen to a doctor on that one.' Emma smiled.

'And I am to "communicate better", she has told me. Something apparently my father failed to do.'

'I'm beginning to like her.' Emma's smile faded;

suddenly she was serious. 'When did you buy my house, Zarios?'

'I put an offer in two days after the funeral.'

'You were with Miranda then.'

'I know.'

'Did you tell her?'

He shook his head. 'I cannot justify or even explain why I did it. I knew it would be tearing you up, having to go through things. I thought if I could just buy it as it was, maybe at some stage… I don't know…'

'You shouldn't have…' Emma gulped. 'On so many levels, you shouldn't have.'

'Don't make me feel guilty for not being open with Miranda—just know that it would never be the same with you. I tried so many times to close the door in my heart to you, and it kept springing open. I wanted to dislike you, to use you as I thought you were using me… Yet I couldn't.'

He was playing with her feet, which she'd always hated. In fact she couldn't imagine letting another person massage her soles or toy with her toes. But she let him.

'I want to see you happy, Emma.'

'I want to see you happy, too.'

'I *am* happy…now that I know you are okay.'

'So the board's decision went your way?'

'Naturally…' He smiled—a different smile, though, a smile she had never seen before, one that made her want to smile, too.

'What?'

'When you are ready to read the newspaper, you will find out that "in a surprising move", I, Zarios D'Amilo—' he spoke in the deadpan voice of a news reporter '—have declined the board's unanimous offer, choosing instead to amalgamate with associates so that I can spend more time with my family. That's you, by the way,' he added in his own voice. 'Just in case you hadn't worked it out. I know it is too soon now for you to be happy—that you haven't had a chance to mourn your parents and that these last months have been hell—but one day I am going to make you happy…'

Tears slid down her face. Only this time she didn't sniff them back. This time she just let them run unchecked, a salty catharsis showing that she didn't have to go it alone any more.

'I just miss them.'

'Of course.'

'I'm glad they never found out about Jake. I'm glad they died thinking he was doing okay. But I wish—I just wish they had lived to find out about *me*. That I'd had more time to make them proud. They'd have been so proud now. Not…' she gulped '…because of how rich you are. I know what I said, what my mother said…'

'They wanted you to be happy, to be secure, and now you are.'

'They don't know that, though. They don't know about the baby, about—'

'Hey.' Now he halted her tears. 'Do you think this is an accident?' His hand crept up to her stomach. 'Can you not see that this is their gift—their way of letting you know that they're okay? Of *course* they know.'

Oh, she wanted to believe that—so badly she wanted to.

'Come here.' He helped her out of bed, and on legs as wobbly as a foal's she was led to her parents' room. 'Look.'

She hadn't been in her parents' bedroom since before they had died, but there, above the balcony doors, was her painting.

'They put it up?' Emma blinked.

'They did,' Zarios lied, hoping she wouldn't notice the edge of the hammer sticking out from under the bed. If she did, he decided then he'd make something up.

It was a good lie—a white lie—and anything was admissible if it made her happy, gave her peace.

'Look closely, Emma.'

And she did.

Looked at the one piece of work in which she'd drawn faces. Her mum and dad, smiling, walking hand in hand along the beach. A laughing couple with a little girl and boy, running ahead. She'd known even as she'd drawn them it was Beth, Jake and the twins.

'How does this help?' She stared at the images her mind had created, and all it did was tear her apart. Every landmark she had known was gone for ever now. 'Beth and Jake are finished.'

'I would have thought so, too; yet she has rung me several times to enquire about him—where he is going, what his treatment will be.'

'It's too big to forgive…'

'I forgave you,' Zarios gently reminded her. 'Not that I needed to, as it turned out, but I *had* worked out that it was easier to forgive you than to lose you. Now, look closer, Emma.'

She frowned, scanning the picture, the surfers and the lady jogging, and the dog swimming in the ocean. Sometimes she hardly recognised her own handiwork, as if she disappeared into another dimension when she worked.

'Look!' Zarios pointed to a couple who were walking, the blonde lady smiling, the tall dark man beside her carrying a little girl on his shoulders, her dark curls dancing. 'That's us.'

'It's just a couple…' Emma protested, but Zarios was adamant.

Pushing her gently down on her parents' bed he held her in his arms as she stared at the picture she had painted—whether it was an image from her mind or a vision of the future she truly didn't know, but there was peace to be had in wondering.

'It's us, Emma…' He stroked the soft mound of her stomach, the gentle heat fading the last remnants of her pain, resting on their baby and telling it to stay for now where it was safe, that they'd meet it when they were all ready. 'That's our family.'

EPILOGUE

'ARE the twins ready…?' Jake's voice trailed off as he walked into the lounge and saw that his wife had company.

'Hi, Emma.' He gave an uncomfortable smile and Emma did the same. 'Zarios.' Jake nodded to his brother-in-law and Zarios nodded back. 'Congratulations.'

'Thank you,' Zarios answered. 'Beth just gave us your gift and card—it is appreciated.'

'You're welcome.'

'Do you want a drink, Jake?' Beth offered, but Jake explained that he couldn't stop. Emma thought that though to many it might seem strange that she and her brother were tonight guests in their late parents' home, on the one-year anniversary of their deaths, it didn't feel strange. It felt right.

Right that even if they weren't here still Eric and Lydia looked after their family—providing Beth and their grandchildren with a comfortable home during these long tumultuous months, a roof over Beth and her children's heads one thing she hadn't had to worry about as her life had rapidly unravelled.

'Well.' Jake gave a wooden smile. 'It's good to see you both—congratulations again.'

The tension was broken a touch as the twins ran into the living room, clearly delighted to see their father. A flurry of kisses and an exchange of bags ensued, as Jake collected his children for his access weekend, but as he turned to go he spoke again.

'Can I see her, Em?'

'Of course…' Emma held her breath as her brother crossed the room and stared down at his niece for the first time.

'Hey, little Lydia.' Jake stroked the petal of her cheek and Emma could see the flash of tears in his eyes. She hated how hard these months had been for him, and that he had lost practically everything—but she was proud of him, too, for turning things around. He had spent four months in rehab, then slowly entered the real world, and as everyone held their breath somehow Jake had held it together. Had found himself work, a flat, and had built from nothing a far gentler life than the one he had previously inhabited.

'Do you want to hold her?'

He did want, and cradled his tiny niece in his arms.

Emma could feel the tears trickling down the back of her nose, and was grateful that Zarios didn't take her hand—because any contact and she would have crumbled.

'You forget how small they are.' Jake looked over to his wife. 'Do you remember—?' He stopped talking then, regret etched on his features as he dragged his gaze back to his niece. Then a ghost of a smile dusted his features. 'It's a good job that you had a girl—I wasn't too keen on having a nephew named Eric!'

'Eric Rocco!' Zarios joined in with the thin joke

as Jake handed Lydia back to her mother. 'I am glad, too, that it was a girl.'

Emma was grateful, too, that Zarios didn't comment on the drive home—just drove quietly as she gazed out of the window, staring out at the view she would love for ever, before daring to voice what she was sure she now knew.

'They're going to get back together.'

'I think so.' Zarios didn't take his eyes off the road.

'What if he slips up? What if—?'

'We'll deal with it as best we can.'

We.

Which was so much stronger than I.

'Thank you…'

Later, much later, when Lydia was bathed and fed and had finished humming herself to sleep in her cot, when they lay exhausted staring at the ceiling, Emma said what she'd been meaning to and thanked Zarios— not just for today, but for the infinite patience he had shown with her family.

'I haven't done anything yet!' Zarios grinned.

'I know it's not been easy with Beth and Jake…'

'Hey, we've got *my* dysfunctional family next weekend…'

He could always make her smile, always make her laugh, always make her want him. His parents lived as if on extended honeymoon, and, as Zarios had pointed out on occasion, if Bella was holding her breath for Rocco to die—well, she was earning her inheritance. His father was the happiest, the healthiest, the youngest he had ever been.

'This year was the worst, and you're through it.' He held her so close she believed him—and tried to come to terms with the fact that the worst year of her life had also, somehow, been the best.

Seeds of hope were budding all around them—love and hope were beckoning from even the darkest of corners.

A chirrup from the cot had them both jumping.

Zarios padded across the floor and didn't even try to scold the twelve-week-old madam who, despite a clean nappy, despite being fed and burped and fed and burped again, had no intention of sleeping.

'Wide awake!' He held up his daughter and black eyes met black eyes, both equally entranced with the other. 'You're ruining my reputation…' He blew raspberries on her fat tummy, making Lydia giggle and coo, before placing her gently back in her cot, to stand the full hour it took before a certain little lady closed her eyes.

'Go to sleep,' he said when, on this most difficult night, Emma turned to him as, cold, tired and beyond exhaustion, he crawled in bed beside her.

'I don't want to.' Smiling, she kissed his full mouth.

She would never let him go.

Would never deny the comfort they brought each other.

She needed this reformed reprobate just as much as he needed her. And knew that, despite a cruel year, life was invariably kind.

After all, they had found each other.

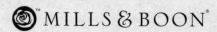

INTERNATIONAL BILLIONAIRES

From rich tycoons to royal playboys –
they're red-hot and ruthless

COLLECT ALL 8 VOLUMES AND COMPLETE THE SET!

Available February 2009

Win
A LUXURY RUGBY
WEEKEND!

see inside books for details

MILLS & BOON
MODERN™
www.millsandboon.co.uk

2 Books
and a surprise gift!

We would like to take this opportunity to thank you for reading this Mills & Boon® book by offering you the chance to take TWO more specially selected titles from the Modern™ series absolutely FREE! We're also making this offer to introduce you to the benefits of the Mills & Boon® Book Club™—

- ★ **FREE home delivery**
- ★ **FREE gifts and competitions**
- ★ **FREE monthly Newsletter**
- ★ **Exclusive Mills & Boon Book Club offers**
- ★ **Books available before they're in the shops**

Accepting these FREE books and gift places you under no obligation to buy, you may cancel at any time, even after receiving your free shipment. Simply complete your details below and return the entire page to the address below. You don't even need a stamp!

YES! Please send me 2 free Modern books and a surprise gift. I understand that unless you hear from me, I will receive 4 superb new titles every month for just £3.19 each, postage and packing free. I am under no obligation to purchase any books and may cancel my subscription at any time. The free books and gift will be mine to keep in any case.

P9ZEF

Ms/Mrs/Miss/Mr ....Initials..............................
BLOCK CAPITALS PLEASE
Surname ....
Address...

....
....Postcode ....

Send this whole page to:
UK: FREEPOST CN81, Croydon, CR9 3WZ